TWICE FREED

TWICE FREED

PATRICIA ST. JOHN

CHRISTIAN FOCUS

Originally published by Pickering and Inglis, Ltd,
26 Bothwell Street, Glasgow, 1970

© copyright 1970 Patricia St. John

This edition printed in 1999 by
Christian Focus Publications
Reprinted 2001, 2002, 2004 and 2006

ISBN 1-85792-489-4; 978-1-85792-489-3

Published by
Christian Focus Publications Ltd
Geanies House, Fearn, Tain, Ross-shire
IV20 1TW, Scotland, Great Britain.
www.christianfocus.com
email: info@christianfocus.com

Cover illustration by M Vinney

Printed and bound by Nørhaven, Denmark

When Patricia St. John was about thirteen years old her imagination was captured by the story of Onesimus, the runaway slave, whose small history was captured in the New Testament book of Philemon. She told our father she wished to write a novel based on the incident, and without a flicker of a smile he accompanied her to the public library.

'My daughter wishes to write a novel set in Bible times,' he announced to the astonished librarian. 'Could you please show her the ancient history section where she can do some research on the period.'

Patricia failed to see the wink that she later felt must have passed between them and felt very solemn and adult. She obediently researched and found out quite a lot about the Roman world and ancient Greece. She wrote her story laboriously, mostly in pencil in a multitude of lined penny notebooks. Our family applauded her but it never went any further. Some years later the manuscript, almost forgotten, was lost in a move.

But the idea never quite left her and one day, years later in 1966, we both set out from Lebanon in a small Volkswagen, with a tent and a primus stove, on a six week journey from Beirut to Tangier in North Africa. This took us to every place mentioned in St. Paul's journeys in the book of Acts and to many other places too, except Caesarea and the islands of the sea. Among the most exciting were Colossae where Onesimus lived, Laodicea across the valley and Rome where through Paul the prisoner Onesimus found new life in Christ.

The story of that journey and it's adventures can be read

in the autobiography *Patricia St. John tells her own Story*, published by STL, *Twice Freed* was written soon after she reached North Africa.

Patricia wrote twenty-six books, mostly for children and teenagers. These have been translated into many different languages. There are also five biographies, a book of verses and the story of the Ruanda Revival, *Breath of life*, and several booklets. Two of her stories, *Treasures of the Snow* and *Tanglewoods Secret* have been made into films, and a third is being prepared.

Though Patricia left us in 1993, letters still come from different parts of the world from grown-ups and children who think she is still with us and who want to tell her how much her stories have meant to them. What always made her most glad was news that someone, through her books, had found like Onesimus the difference that knowing Christ can make to life.

Dedicated
to my sister Hazel
who produced a Volkswagen and
a tent and accompanied me
in the steps of St. Paul

Patricia St. John

1

IT WAS MID AFTERNOON IN EARLY JULY AND the parched world was, in general asleep.

The black flocks, for which the valley was famous, huddled under the poplar trees, and the reapers drowsed in the shade of their stooks of corn or under their wooden carts.

In the well-to-do houses, set high above the pasture land, prosperous land owners and farmers and wool merchants slept soundly on their couches, while their slaves dozed guiltily, with one ear cocked, under the vines in the courtyard. Even the vultures hung motionless as though stuck flat against the blue.

Only up in the gorge, where the air seemed to swim over the burning rocks, something moved. A brown-skinned boy of twelve, naked except for a loin cloth and sandals, was climbing the canyon with the grace and agility of a young wild cat. He cared nothing for the sweat that was streaming down his face or for the rocks that blistered his hands, for this was his hour of freedom. From early dawn till late at night he belonged to his master and outwardly bowed to his discipline; but at this hour he belonged to himself and lived and conquered and exulted.

Here in the canyons nothing could withstand him. In winter he cut paths through the snow drifts, and in spring he breasted the cascades and the waterfalls. In summer the fierce afternoon heat could not daunt him and he climbed on, with one eye on the sun which was now to the west of him. When the shadow of the rock above him reached the border of the olive grove below, he knew he must turn home. But he still had time to reach the old fallen pine that blocked the ravine, and to dive into the green pool that lay on the further side of it.

The gorge was narrowing now, and the pines and stunted oaks and junipers cast their shade across the ravine. The stream was no more than a trickle, but it was cool and sweet, and he dashed the water over his face and body and felt he could go on climbing all day. He always yearned to go further - up to the bitter salt lake, Anava, where the absinthe flowers grew and where the river Lycus was born, up to the snows of Mount Cadmus - but the shade was creeping toward the olive grove, and his master would be stirring in his sleep. He cursed and spat.

At least he would have time for a quick swim in the green pool that was so deep that it never dried up. He scrambled up on to the fallen tree, and then stopped dead, his mouth open and his eyes dilated with a strange superstitious fear. For a little girl was sitting on the trunk, dangling her legs over the water, singing softly to herself.

She was about nine or ten years old, small and slender, with smooth dark hair hanging to her waist. Her cheeks were flushed with heat, and her lap was full of the flowers she had been gathering - drooping scabious and buttercups and forget-me-nots from the stream's edge. So absorbed was she that she did not see the boy approaching.

Who was she? Her simple tunic was of rich material, her sandals were new and expensive. Her bearing, even as she played, was that of a little queen. He watched her intently, crouching on the trunk, for he was still not sure of her identity. Was she some daughter of Cybele, the great mother of Nature, to whose arms the dead returned like homing children? Well, if she was, there was nothing to fear, for she was certainly no demon. He drew a little nearer, and a twig snapped under his feet.

She looked up and gave a start but she showed no great surprise or fear. For she was a practical child, and to her a boy was a boy. Besides, he looked a nice boy, and she was just beginning to feel slightly afraid of what she had done.

"What are you doing up here, boy?" she asked, in perfect Greek. "I thought everyone was asleep."

"What are you doing?" he retorted rather severely, for he was convinced now that she was nothing but a human girl. "It is a long way up the canyon for a little maid to stray alone. And, anyway, who are you?"

"I'm Eirene," replied the child. She spoke guardedly and watched him gravely, as though wondering how much it was safe to reveal. And he gazed back at her, the tremulous sunlight falling upon her through the pine boughs, so alone and defenceless among the crags of the ravine; and he found himself longing to know all about her, to gain her trust and, if need be, to protect her.

"But where is your home, Eirene? I've never seen you playing with the little girls of Colosse."

"I live in Laodicea," she replied, still watchful, still hesitant.

"Laodicea!" he repeated in astonishment, for Laodicea

11

was ten miles across the valley. "Surely you never came here alone, and will no one be looking for you?"

"Yes, they will!" Her eyes suddenly twinkled with amusement, and her confidences came pouring out. "They will be getting crazy about me. I came over this morning with my father. He makes cloaks, and he came to talk to Master Philemon about wool. But they went in to dine together, and I was left with my nurse and the slaves. My nurse started to talk to Philemon's slaves, and she didn't want me to hear. She gave me some food and told me to go out into the vineyard, but there was nothing to do in the vineyard. I wanted to climb and see what lay at the top of the canyons, so I ran away. I climbed right up here, and I should have gone further, but the green pool stopped me."

"But weren't you afraid, so high up, all alone?"

"No," replied Eirene with spirit. "I like being alone. I get sick of my nurse. She is so afraid of my father she never takes her eyes off me at home. It is Eirene this, Eirene that, till I could scream. Why should I do what she wants and go where she takes me, all day long? Don't you ever want to get away from everybody and do what you like, instead of doing what you are told all the time?"

The boy laughed aloud. Here was indeed a kindred spirit!

"Yes," he replied, "indeed I do. That is why I come up the ravine: to get away from everyone and do what I like. Sometimes, when I have time, I swim across the pools and go higher up into the rocks, up to where the eagles live. One day I shall go even further. One day I shall follow the river right to its source. One day I shall climb right to the top of the peak and look over the whole land of Phrygia and away to the sea westward. And then one day, I shall cross that sea. They say the land of Greece is the most beautiful in the world."

He stopped, surprised at his own outburst, for he usually kept his longing to himself. His thoughts came back abruptly to the little creature at his side, who sat staring up at him, eyes alight, sharing his visions.

"You ought to go home!" he said. "Your nurse will be out of her mind. And what about your mother? Did you leave her in Laodicea?"

A shadow passed over the child's face. "She died two years ago," she said simply. "When she was alive it was different. She never watched me all the time. She let me play, pick flowers and go where I liked. When she was alive, I was free."

"Have you no brothers or sisters to play with?"

"No, there's only me. My father says I am all he has and very precious to him; so my nurse never dares to stop looking after me. My father is a very busy man, always down at the looms, or going to look at wools, or travelling down to Ephesus or Miletus with his merchandise. Sometimes I think he forgets all about me."

"I don't suppose he does really," said the boy, comfortingly. "Come, Eirene, we must go home now, at once. Swing over the bough like that and you will reach the rock with the tips of your toes. Now, down to the next one and into the stream bed. It is easier there. Loop you dress into your girdle and take my hand. Now just jump from rock to rock as I do, and we'll soon be down."

He glanced anxiously at the shadows below him. Already half the olive grove was immersed in shade. He was very late, and his master Philemon had an important guest and would have been yelling for him for the past hour. He had not known what had been happening in his master's house, as he had been sent out early with a message to the shepherds in a distant pasture up the valley, and he had not been expected back until after Philemon's siesta. Perhaps he could invent some story about difficulty in finding the flocks. That might at least delay his beating until his master could investigate. In any case it did not matter too much. He was used to beatings. What mattered now was the nimble little creature who held his hand so rightly and laughed so gaily is she missed her footing, skipping from one side of the stream bed to the other. He must hand her over safe and sound to her nurse.

And say goodbye? She was the only daughter of a rich Laodicean merchant and he a poor slave at Colosse. Why should his mind refuse so doggedly to say goodbye? They were nearly out of the canyon now, and he reached up to help her down from a boulder too high for her. But before he could take hold of her he was startled by a piercing scream behind him, and turning his head quickly, he received a stinging slap in the face then another and another from a strong young slave, while the nurse screamed hysterically and held out her arms to the child.

"Oh, Mistress Eirene, Mistress Eirene, you cruel girl," shrieked the nurse. "How could you disobey me and run off with this wicked, wicked boy? Oh, Mistress Eirene, I've been nearly out of my mind, hunting through the vineyards where I told you to stay. How could you listen to a low slave and run away from your own poor nurse?

Oh, beat him again, Menander, beat the breath out of him!"

Menander, holding the boy fast, noticed that he neither struggled nor made any attempt to escape. He lifted his hand to strike him again but was arrested by a sudden shriek of rage above him. Eirene stood poised on the boulder like a small commanding fury, her eyes blazing, trembling with anger.

"Let him go this instant, Menander," she shouted. "Do as I tell you immediately or I'll tell my father of you. How dare you hit that good boy?"

She suddenly ceased to be a commanding fury and burst into tears, a frightened hurt little girl whose happy afternoon had been spoilt. Kicking her nurse aside, she slid off the boulder all by herself and took her stand defiantly beside the boy.

Menander had let go. He had a healthy fear of his little mistress' temper.

"Does my father know I'm lost yet?" asked Eirene, sniffing hard. The tears were still running down her cheeks, but she had drawn herself up to her full small height and held her head high.

"No, Mistress Eirene," twittered the nurse. "He is still talking business, but he will call for you at any moment now. I pray you come back quickly."

"I shall not come back if you say any bad things about this boy," retorted Eirene. "I shall stay here and be lost, and my father will be very, very angry with you both for losing me. He will probably punish you both when I tell him."

It was only too likely. The nurse started to plead tearfully. Menander scratched his head. The boy looked her straight in the face.

"Come home, Eirene," he said gently. "I must go to my work now; but if I see your father I will tell him you are all coming." He took her hand and helped her over the last rough bit of rock. Menander controlled himself with difficulty.

"Mistress," protested the frantic nurse, "a common slave..."

"I don't care what he is," retorted Eirene. "He's a boy, and he helped me. Goodbye, boy, and thank you. One day we will meet again."

"The gods forbid," muttered Menander under his breath; but the boy took no notice. He turned back and looked straight at Eirene and spoke to her alone, as though ratifying a covenant. "Yes," he said, "one day we shall meet again."

2

HE SPED DOWN THE STEEP OLIVE SLOPES AND arrived breathless at his master's house. He had not wanted Eirene to know he was Philemon's slave, but, of course, it had all come out in the end. It always did, he thought suddenly. There was no escaping the fact of his slavery. And yet it had not really mattered. It warmed his heart that, knowing all, she had still stood by him and still wanted to see him again. The thought of that had made him forget his stinging bruised cheeks; in fact he only remembered them as he flung himself breathlessly into his master's house and confronted young Archippus, Philemon's son.

"You're late, Onesimus," said Archippus sharply. "My father has been calling for you. He has a guest, and he wanted you to bring the wine when they finished the siesta. He is very displeased with you. Where have you been and who slapped you in the face?"

"I've been down at the sheep pastures," said Onesimus hopefully. "It took a long time to find those shepherds. They had gone down to the river to water the flocks."

"Liar!" said Archippus scornfully. "You were back from the pastures soon after noon. One of the slaves saw you running up to those precious ravines of yours several hours ago, and my father knows it; so don't try this story out on him."

It was only two or three years ago that Onesimus and Archippus had climbed the canyons together, and although Archippus, since leaving school, was busy establishing the new relationship of master and slave, and Onesimus was busy resenting it, there was still a close bond between them. Archippus as a baby had spent hours in the slaves' hut, watching the grindstone, blowing on the charcoal, snuggling down into the unteazled piles of black sheeps-wool that awaited the spinning-wheel. The two had explored the stream beds together, dammed the same pools, shared secrets about birds' nests and foxes' lairs and together tracked bears and hyenas. Onesimus hated Archippus and was ashamed of it, because Archippus had been his good friend in the past. Archippus loved Onesimus and was also ashamed of it. It was weak and unmanly to love a slave.

"Who is the guest?" asked Onesimus, hastily wiping the mud off his hands and arms and slipping on a clean tunic.

"Polemon, from Laodicea," replied Archippus impressively. "He's the richest cloak-maker in the town, and he has decided to buy our wool. He came over this morning to see some of our flocks and to take back samples. He may even introduce our wool to others of his guild. It may mean a journey to Ephesus later on, and I shall go too."

Onesimus, fastening his girdle, made no reply. Somewhat fearfully he entered the atrium or central court of the house and stood before his master. Archippus, anxious to see what would happen slipped in behind him and sat down at his father's feet.

Philemon and his guest reclined on couches, sipping

their wine and talking eagerly. It was a beautiful courtyard, shaded by an old vine which dangled its ripe bunches of grapes through the lattice work that supported it. The floor was paved in the Greek style with coloured mosaic, and a fountain played in the centre. Philemon, a prosperous farmer, with a keen, weather-bronzed face, turned sharply on the young truant. His guest was an important one, and though he had plenty of slaves on call, he would have liked to have had this graceful boy in attendance.

"Why are you late?" he asked coldly.

It suddenly struck Onesimus that it might pay to tell the truth, or at least some of it. It might also afford an excellent opportunity of revenging himself on the slave Menander. He turned and bowed to the guest.

"I beg you to excuse me, Sir", he said. "You have a little daughter?"

Philemon frowned, and the guest raised his eyebrows, as much as to say, "If I have, what is that to you?"

"She strayed too far at her play, Sir," went on Onesimus undiscouraged. "I saw her climbing the rocks up in the ravines and went after her. She was little, Sir, and the boulders were high. I brought her down slowly, helping her where the ground was rough."

"And in the name of the goddess," exclaimed Polemon the cloak-maker, half rising, "where was her nurse? And where is Eirene now?"

"I restored her to her nurse, master," replied Onesimus. "In fact I met the nurse and the slave Menander at the entrance to the vineyards searching for her. No harm has come to the little maid. If you would have me bring her..."

19

"I will go myself," said Archippus rising hastily, "and see that all is well." His handsome young face was flushed with jealousy and arrogance. That impudent young Onesimus should have been keeping company with Polemon's daughter and championing her in danger was indeed a twist of fortune. He left the room hastily, and Polemon carelessly threw a piece of gold at Onesimus.

"Take that for your services," he said. "The nurse shall be dismissed tonight and the slave punished. She's a wilful little maid and needs a mother. Now, to go back to those bales of wool we were discussing just now......"

His daughter was forgotten and he was once again intent on his money-making, his eyes gimlet-shrewd. Onesimus stood quietly at attention for a time, pouring out wine when necessary, and then Philemon sent him to fetch fruit, and he left the room on silent bare feet.

But as he crossed the outer courtyard on his way to the kitchen, he stopped and caught his breath. Eirene was sitting in front of the house, framed in the vine leaves that clustered round the door. She was playing with a late-born black lamb that Archippus had brought her, and he sat beside her, both of them laughing at the tame nuzzling little creature. Her nurse was on guard a short distance away. As Onesimus came toward them, Eirene looked up and called to him joyously. He took a step towards her, smiling, but Archippus rose immediately.

"Back to your work, slave," he ordered, and Onesimus had no choice but to obey his master's son. Ashamed to look again at the happy, innocent little face, he hurried on his errand, and it was not till he was standing again behind his master that he realised that something had happened to him. In those few moments he had changed.

Firstly, all his allegiance to the memory of their childhood together had died, and he now hated Archippus with a steady, purposeful hatred. Secondly, he had made up his mind to be free. At whatever cost, and whatever he had to do to achieve it, he would be free. He fingered his small gold piece knotted in his girdle, and it seemed like a pledge.

"I will keep it till I purchase my freedom," he said to himself. "It is the beginning."

"Slave!" Philemon spoke sharply and clapped his hands. "I have spoken, and you take no heed! Fetch Master Polemon's cloak and give word to the slaves to prepare his litter."

The slaves were already waiting, glancing anxiously at the westering sun; for they had ten miles to go, and the valley abounded in thieves and robbers lying in wait for rich travellers after sunset. Onesimus helped Polemon into his cloak and put on his sandals, and then withdrew to watch the departure from behind the lintel of the stables. He saw Archippus lift the little girl into the seat beside her father and hand her a vine leaf of mulberries, and he noticed that she thanked him gravely and politely, but with eyes averted; nor did she say "We shall meet again." As the four slaves set off at a run with the gorgeous litter borne on their shoulders, he saw her lean out and take a long look back, but she was not looking for Archippus. He wondered why, for Archippus was strong and handsome, two years older than himself and half a head taller.

By the time he had cleared up the remains of the midday banquet and laid out the evening meal and mixed the wine with honey, it was nearing sunset. Another slave would wait on the family while they ate, and he was free to go home. As he rose at cock-crow he was usually ready to swallow his food and fall asleep; but tonight he was in no hurry and sleep seemed far from him. He sat in the doorway, long after he had finished his supper of lentils, looking out to where the sun had now dipped behind the mountains north-west of the valley and the colours still flamed in the sky. On the upper plain of Colosse the harvest was nearly ended and the slow wooden wagons, drawn by oxen, were rumbling up the dusty paths between the poplars, the tired reapers resting on the piled up wheat. Behind them across the valley he could see the white limestone cliffs and cascades of Hierapolis, and below them, on the grassy hill above the river, the roofs and columns of Laodicea.

Perhaps she would have arrived by now. All the little sounds of twilight, the croaking of the frogs in the marsh, the whirr of crickets, the rattling cry of the stork making for her nest, the bleating of the folded sheep, seemed clearer and more important than ever before. He stared with rapt attention at the curling tendrils of the vine leaf, the crimson folded petals of the pomegranate flowers within reach of his hand, and he knew again he had changed.

"Mother," he said suddenly, "tell me about my father."

His mother laughed and sat down beside her moody, restless son, her hands busy with the studded teazing card, her heart with him all the time. She was a beautiful dark-eyed Phrygian woman, born into slavery, content with a master who was kind as masters went. She had loved her husband dearly, but she was glad that death had set him free, for to him slavery was a bondage too heavy to be borne.

"I think you know all there is to be known," she said. "What ails you tonight?"

He shook his head. "Nothing," he replied. "Only I should like to hear again about my father."

"He was born on the slopes of Mount Parnassus in Greece," began his mother, "and he loved all beautiful things. When he grew up he became a scholar in Athens. He said it was the most beautiful city in the world, and often he would sit of an evening and talk to me about his country. He would go on and on about islands set like jewels in a blue sea, about mountains whose heads were veiled in clouds where the gods lived, and about the great marble Acropolis standing on a hill above the city. He married me because I was beautiful and he loved me; but he was never happy here in a strange land and among strange gods. Those born free cannot submit to slavery. It was well that he returned to Cybele and her fair meadows." She fell silent, gazing out into the dusk.

"Go on," said Onesimus. "Tell me about the brigands."

"Your father was a traveller, always restless, always wanting to see over the top of the mountain," said his mother with a tender smile. "He lectured for years in a school in Athens and then set off one early spring to visit the University of Tarsus and to study the teaching of one, Athenodorus. He often talked about that journey. He joined a caravan in early summer when the snows were melting on the Taurus mountains. How he loved the gazelles on the Cilician plains! At the end of the summer he travelled on, while the roads into Syria were still open, and wintered in Jerusalem."

"Did he tell you much about Jerusalem?"

"Yes. Many a winter night he would sit by the fire and talk about Jerusalem; for he arrived at a strange time, some twenty-six years ago. The Romans had not long before crucified a man called Jesus, hated by the Jewish rulers, but greatly loved by the common people."

"Why did the rulers hate him?"

"They feared him, and he taught some new religion. But although they had crucified him, Jerusalem that winter was full of his followers. There were strange stories afloat too. Hundreds had declared that he had risen from the dead and claimed that they had actually seen him. Besides, there was something about his followers that made people afraid of them. They possessed a strange power. Your father actually saw one of them take hold of a well-known lame beggar and command him in the name of Jesus to rise up and walk, and the man ran into the Jews' temple leaping and shouting. They did not seem to mind being persecuted either."

"But why were they persecuted? Did they do wrong?"

"No, they were full of good works; but their teaching would have turned the world upside down. They taught a brotherhood between Jew and Gentile, slave and free. They made no difference. Naturally the upper classes and the Jewish leaders opposed it."

"Did my father accept this teaching?"

"No. He had his own gods and goddesses who lived on Parnassus, gods of thunder and gods of war and goddesses of hunting. His favourite, I believe, was the goddess of beauty, for he used to say he found her everywhere: in the sunsets, in the first spring flowers, in the vine tendrils. But he stayed for some months in Jerusalem, and just before he left he saw something he never forgot. One of the followers of Jesus, called Stephanos, was on trial for his life. He was brought into the council as the result of some street brawl and your father was in the crowd. Stephanos was given a fair chance to defend himself, but he seemed not to care whether he lived or died provided he could say what he believed about this Jesus. The mob got angry in the end - began shrieking and cursing, but he never even seemed to see them. He was looking up into the sky, his face alight like the face of a god. He said something but your father could not hear. Later, one standing near vowed that he had cried out, 'I see the Heaven opened and Jesus standing at the right hand of God'. Anyhow, the crowd all went mad and fell on him and dragged him outside the city and started to stone him. He looked up again and called to someone, but he was soon beaten down. Only just before he died, he seemed to be asking his god to forgive his murderers."

"To forgive his murderers?" Onesimus suddenly laughed. "I don't believe it."

"Yet it was true. Having heard him, your father never forgot."

"Then that Stephanos was a poor fool. Tell me about the brigands."

"Your father lingered in Jerusalem and left the journey home too late. The first rains fell as he passed through the dark Cilician gates. He was benighted with his companions, and the brigands came swooping down from the Taurus mountains. They took everything: his money, his clothes and, what he minded most, his precious books. He himself was taken captive and sold as a slave in a Phyrgian market."

"And then," said Onesimus softly, "he met you."

"My master paid a high price for him because he was young and strong and handsome, and he married me who had been born on the estate. I comforted him and bore him children, but life was hard on those high, desolate plains, and the first three died. Your father was never a good slave; nothing could tame his fierce Greek pride."

"And then I was born."

"Yes, you were born, and the end came quite soon. Our master was determined to break him, making him work for long hours in the deep Cilician mud when he was weakened by coughing and fever. Then one day he ordered him to beat a child slave who had accidentally broken something, and your father refused. Our master struck him, and your father struck back. He never rose again from his bed after the punishment they gave him, although day after day in his fever, he prayed the gods to give him strength to revenge his injuries. Then on the night he died ... it was very strange. He talked about Stephanos. 'How could a man die without fear and without hatred?' he asked me. 'How could a man ask forgiveness for his murderers? Whom did Stephanos see?' Many times he asked the question, but I could give him no answer. At dawn he died."

"And then?"

"Soon after that the gods executed vengeance, and our master fell from his horse while hunting and was killed by a wild boar. We were all sold again, and fate was kind. You and I were bought together and, my son, you should praise the gods for a just master."

"Why should I have a master at all?" said the boy obstinately.

His mother laughed gently and ran her fingers through his thick dark hair. "You were born like your father to love beauty and freedom, more's the pity. But tonight I will tell you something I have never told you before. Every coin I can earn or steal I am hiding away for you to buy your freedom. One day you will be free."

He fingered the gold piece knotted in his girdle, and a wild hope surged up in his heart. One day he would be free, free to wander, free to hate and to revenge himself, free to love.

He stared out into the night sky to where the first stars burned over Laodicea.

3

AFTER THAT THE BURNING SUMMER DAYS seemed to race past, and Onesimus worked from dawn to dusk. The wheat harvest was nearly in, and there were rejoicings on the threshing floor, sacrifices and processions. And before the grain was stored in the underground pits, the grapes were ripe for vintage. Gangs of slaves worked all day long in the vineyards, picking the grapes, spreading them out to dry, carrying them in great cart-loads to the winepress, pruning the vines and holding high festivals to Bacchus.

It was a merry time of year and Onesimus loved it. By the time they started to gather the figs and pomegranates the poplars in the upper plain were beginning to turn golden along with the bracken that clothed the lower hillsides. The air was heady and sweet as good wine, and every house top was gay with its store of raisins, figs, corn and pomegranates drying in the sunshine. Cool and clear were the mornings, with mists rising from the river in the valley and all the trees heavy with fruit. It seemed as if their mother, Cybele, was pouring out showers of gifts on her children in prodigal wasteful abundance, as a last token of her blessing, before the dark wintry days should come.

But before they were through with the olive harvest, well before the oil was stored, the first snows were flurrying down the ravines, and the conical peak at the east of the glen and the towering head of Cadmus were powdered with snow. Winds were beginning to howl round the canyons and across the plains, and winter was upon them, with jackals and hyenas howling in the gorges, with the rain and mud, the silence of the snow, and the angry crimson sunsets down the valley.

The rich lit their great heating braziers, and slaves were kept busy piling on the charcoal. But the slaves themselves, in their leaking mud huts, fared ill. The great roads to the East were blocked by snow, and no travellers passed by, and no news reached them from the outer world. There was little to do and nothing to talk about except the bitter cold and the old slaves' rheumatism.

But there came a day when Onesimus went out at dawn and heard the bleating of the first young lambs and felt a breath of warm south wind stealing down from the high passes, and he knew that on the other side of the mountains the sea was blue. He looked down and saw a clump of dwarf narcissi flowering in mud. Spring was on the way. Very soon the spring ploughing and sowing would begin, and the storks would arrive from Syria.

Everyone stirred to the breath of the south wind. The sun shone out and the snows began to melt. The cascades overflowed their banks, half flooding the meadows as they foamed to the valley. Ships began to cross the sea, and the roads were once again thronged with merry travellers bringing tales from East and West. Mistress Apphia, Philemon's wife, took advantage of the fine weather to spring-clean her mansion, and so there was plenty of work to do, and little Pascasia, her daughter, adopted a motherless lamb and nursed it like a baby.

"We are going over to Laodicea next week," said Archippus carelessly one spring evening, pausing at the door of the stable where Onesimus was cleaning and polishing his master's riding equipment. "My father and I are both to be fitted with a new trimiton at Master Polemon's establishment, and I am to have new sandals. I will give you my old ones, Onesimus."

Onesimus acknowledged his favour as ungraciously as he dared. He could not understand Archippus these days. He was growing at an alarming rate and at fifteen was almost as tall as his father, and he alternated between snubbing and humiliating Onesimus in every possible way and then seeking him out and trying to regain their old comradeship and offering him presents. But he might as well have tried to be friendly with a brick wall, and he little knew how every slight and wounding word was being stored up in the boy's memory. Archippus had become to him the symbol of his slavery, and he hated him with all the strength of his proud young heart.

Archippus sighed. He longed to possess this boy wholly and to gain his devotion and respect and admiration; but when they were together something always whispered that it was hopeless. He rose, knowing himself defeated, but still he lingered.

"I have to take a chain of my mother's down to the goldsmith's for repair," he said at last. "Be ready to accompany me in an hour's time."

As they sauntered down the road towards the town, Onesimus' black mood lightened, for the beauty of the early spring days always moved and lifted him. The almond blossom twisting from the naked wood and the gold of the dandelions along the roadside made even

Archippus seem less odious, and had he been alone he would have run and leaped and praised the gods. As it was, he walked, as befitted a slave, two or three paces behind his young master, obstinately refusing Archippus' invitation to forget the relationship and walk together.

"I hope my father will take you in attendance tomorrow," said Archippus generously. "The streets of Laodicea are a real sight after the dull little streets of Colosse, and they say that Master Polemon lives in a marble mansion. Little Mistress Eirene no doubt will have grown throughout the winter. I must take her some little gift."

A small cloud passed over the face of the sun, and Onesimus trudged on in silence!

"The messenger who came to summon us to Laodicea brought news of the world beyond Colosse," went on Archippus with a little laugh. "In Thyatira the dye merchants are complaining about the Jewish settlers; the new Emperor, Nero, flourishes in Rome, and no Emperor has ever lived so gloriously or in more royal style; down in Ephesus the Greek traders and the local silversmiths have been rioting in the streets again. The priests are anxious for the honour of their goddess and not only on account of the competition of trade. There are rumours of a strange new teaching that seems to be taking root everywhere, the teaching of some Jewish peasant who died by crucifixion in his own capital. It is strange how ignorant people will fall for every new-fangled ridiculous fable they hear."

"Jesus," said Onesimus, startled into speech. "They say he rose again from the dead."

"Where and from whom did you hear that?" asked

Archippus, turning round sharply. Onesimus' frequent knowledge of subjects about which he himself often knew nothing had always annoyed him.

"I hear these things," replied Onesimus lightly; for the memory of his father was a wound he had never shown to Archippus.

"Well, they say the teaching has already taken root in Hierapolis," went on Archippus. "A native of our own city, Colosse, who has been working with some tent-makers at Ephesus, has been wintering there. The followers of Jesus are making quite a stir. They cease to fear the demons or to offer sacrifices, and they worship one invisible God - Jews and Carians, Greeks and Phrygians all mixed up together like a lot of silly tame sheep. They say that the temple priests as well as the Jews have tried to suppress the movement, but these people are patient under persecutions. One of their maxims is to love and forgive their enemies. That is what that crucified peasant leader of theirs did."

"Well I don't want to love or forgive my enemies," said Onesimus with quiet finality, and the two boys fell silent until they reached the town.

It was a prosperous little town, centred on its wool market and its purple dye works. On the outskirts stood a fast-growing Jewish colony with its isolated, unpopular community. The boys sauntered through the streets, lingering near the open-fronted shops. Delicious smells came from the cooked meat shops, and merry crowds jostled with each other at the entrance of the wine shops. Watered gardens with marble statues lay between the streets where children ran and shouted, playing hopscotch or bowling their hoops. They passed the temple and the school where Archippus had once learned reading and writing and mathematics, Latin and Greek. It was always a source of wonder to Onesimus, who would have given almost anything to learn to read, that Archippus had persuaded his father to take him away from school so early.

"Geometry, astronomy, philosophy and music!" he had exclaimed to Onesimus. "What good will they ever do me? I want to learn to take over my father's farm and trade and make money and travel. Am I not his only son?" And since this was an argument that had appealed to Philemon, Archippus had left school at thirteen and two years later was already showing himself an able overseer with a flair for money-making.

The goldsmith's shop was in a small side street, and they found him intent on heating his gold in a little crucible that looked like an egg shell. Heating and refining, heating and refining, he crouched over his furnace absorbed in his work, till the seven times purified liquid showed him his own face as in a mirror. The boys, unwilling to interrupt him, stood waiting. Archippus stared thoughtfully at an exquisite little chain and pendant.

"I should like to hang that round the little white throat of Mistress Eirene," he said. "And see, Onesimus, these bracelets - what cunning craftsmanship! And these curios, little figures of the gods!" He roamed restlessly round the shop, but Onesimus stood still, watching the bubbling metal and the skilled hands of the craftsman purging the gold of its dross.

At last the old man looked up, and Archippus handed him the broken necklace and explained what his mother wanted done. Very respectfully, the goldsmith promised to have it ready next day; for Philemon was one of his richest clients, and he was pleased that Philemon's son should have honoured his little shop by coming in person. He would have asked many questions concerning the health and welfare of his patron's establishment, but Archippus seemed eager to leave the shop. Instead of lingering to watch the bales of wool being unloaded, or to listen to a wandering street musician, he hurried on at a round pace, until the two boys were once more on the steep track that led to their upland farm.

"What is the hurry, master?" asked Onesimus in surprise, pausing for breath at the bottom of the hill.

"You should be back at your work," replied Archippus. "My father will be needing you. Come, don't dawdle about."

He was already hurrying ahead when Onesimus called to him.

"Stop, master. Wait. Someone is riding after us and shouting at us, an old man, by the way he rides. Why, it is the goldsmith, mounted like a sack on an old mule, waving his whip as though some disaster had happened! He will fall off if he drives that poor old beast any faster." Then, suddenly, he stopped laughing, for Archippus was standing grave and irresolute, and his face was very white.

"Stupid old man," he muttered. "Whatever can he want? Let us go on, Onesimus, and take no note of him."

"But, master," said the slave, "he will catch us up in no time, unless he breaks his neck first." And indeed the old man had already left the town behind and was careering up the slope, beating the mule for all he was worth. His head-dress was all askew, and he was clutching the mule by the mane. Onesimus, without further ado, ran to meet him and was just in time to catch him as he slithered off sideways.

"Can I help you, father?" asked Onesimus. "Has anything happened?"

"Let me speak to your master," cried the old man. He was trembling with shock and seemed half distraught. "Ah, young master, come hither. What is this that you boys have done? The chain and locket, it is gone! Shame on you to trick an old man so!"

There was a moment's silence. Just for a second Archippus seemed uncertain what to reply. Then he spoke, and his voice was haughty.

"We know nothing of your chain, Master Plautus. Maybe some other customer . . .!

"There was no other customer," cried the old man, wringing his hands. "Do you think I do not know my gold as a father knows his children? Could one piece be missing and I would not know it with my whole soul and body? Oh, you are fleet-footed, but you cannot escape me!" He was trembling all over. "Unless that chain is restored, I will walk beside you to the house of Master Philemon and search you both in his presence. Ah me, do you not fear the gods that you should do this to a poor old man?"

"Peace, Master Plautus," said Archippus quietly. "There is no need to take you so far up the hill. Already your ride has been too much for you. You may search us here on the path. I will search my slave here in your presence, and then you are at liberty to search me."

He took hold of Onesimus rather roughly and dragged him into the middle of the path. At the same time he shouted, "Look to your mule, Master Plautus."

The animal, unnoticed, was making off quietly toward home. The goldsmith hobbled a few steps down the path and returned, dragging the beast by its bridle. He was dizzy and breathless, bewildered between watching the boys and fear of a sudden bite from the mule. Archippus passed his hands carefully over Onesimus' person, removed his sandals, shook out his cloak. Then he removed his thick girdle, and as he did so the gold chain fell to the ground and lay sparkling in the sun in full view of them all.

4

THERE WAS A MOMENT'S STUNNED silence, and both boys stood rooted to the spot. Then the old man pounced on his gold with a triumphant scream and stood there fondling it and gloating over it. Then he lifted his skinny old hands to Heaven and began to call down the curses of the gods on the thief.

"That is enough, Master Plautus," said Archippus. He tried to speak with authority, but his voice shook slightly. "You have your trinket, and I will take my slave home and see that justice is administered. I assure you that the punishment will be all he deserves."

"A branding," shouted the old man, shaking his fist feebly at Onesimus. "It must be a branding. That I demand. I myself will come in person and see it carried out. I don't trust boys. Let me speak to his master myself. I will be content with nothing but a branding."

"Go home, Master Plautus," entreated Archippus, drawing up the mule and trying to persuade the old man to mount it. "I will mention the matter of a branding to my father, as you wish, and he will decide. I assure you he is not one to let a dishonest thief get off lightly. Justice will be administered. Come slave!" He pushed Onesimus ahead of him with a rather unsteady hand and started off up the hill.

But the old man had no intention of leaving this

affair to Archippus. Passion made him strong, and with a tremendous effort he pulled himself up onto his beast and came lumbering up the hill on their heels, cursing, slobbering at the mouth, trembling with exertion and excitement.

"Branding," the goldsmith was muttering the word over and over again, the mark of a thief, burned indelibly on the forehead of a slave, proclaiming his disgrace and his slavery till the day of his death. No man with that mark could ever again hold up his head among free men. And Onesimus was thirteen. He had a long way to go.

A wild idea of flight seized him, and he looked round in desperation. But there was nowhere to flee to. The upper plain stretched for miles, with no hope of a hiding place, and that wretched old bag of bones puffing along on the mule behind him would soon track him in the town. He would be pursued and caught like a wild beast if he fled to the canyons. Only death could shelter him now, and how gladly would he have embraced death, but where was death to be found? The foaming river was a mile away, and he had no weapon. "Oh, ye gods, ye gods, if gods there be," he cried from the depths of his terrified heart, "oh father of gods, and Artemis our mother, not branding, oh, not branding."

Trembling, white, driven by Archippus up the hill, Onesimus now reached Philemon's mansion. Archippus gave brief orders to an older slave to put a chain on the boy, and then without a word or backward glance he went to find his father. The old man seemed unable to dismount and was only restrained with difficulty from shambling in on his mule, right into Philemon's private apartment.

They stood waiting. Apart from the babbling of the old man, it was very quiet. Pigeons cooed in the nesting-boxes at the side of the house; a small slave girl passed by on an errand and gave Onesimus a quick compassionate glance. Her slender little figure and dark tresses reminded him of another, and quick tears started to his eyes. What if *she* should see him with the mark of the brand on his forehead? But he must not weep in front of Archippus; that was the most important thing of all. With difficulty he lifted up his chained hands and wiped away his tears.

And then a slave appeared at the door of the outer courtyard and bade the party enter. Seeing the mule joining the procession, he helped the exhausted old man dismount and half dragged him, half carried him into the presence of Philemon.

Philemon sat in the doorway of his apartment which opened into the atrium, and behind him in the shadows his wife, Apphia, was stitching at her embroidery, the golden Phrygian embroidery, famous all over the Roman world. Her five-year-old daughter, Pascasia, played at her feet. Archippus, half hidden behind a pillar, stood waiting on his father. Onesimus saw these things in a dream, and even the babblings of the old man now seemed far away and unreal. He hardly heard what he said nor cared that all eyes were upon him as he stood there, young and pitiful and in chains. Only his heart kept calling out, "Not branding, not branding," but to whom he called, or whether there was any to hear, he did not really know.

"So you see, my noble master," finished up the old man, suddenly falling flat at Philemon's feet, whether from reverence or exhaustion no one quite knew, "he must be branded. Let us heat the irons that I may witness the punishment and be off to my humble home. I am a poor man, master. If you would grant me a slight token of your favour..."

Philemon glanced at the prostrate goldsmith with extreme distaste and then turned to the white-faced boy in fetters and gazed at him thoughtfully. Onesimus had grown up with his own son and had tumbled round his footstool in babyhood. He was surprised at his own reluctance to sentence this slave, but discipline must be maintained and branding was the usual punishment for thieves.

"Very well," he said rather wearily, "he shall be branded. Janus go and heat the irons and take the boy where my wife cannot hear his screams."

All eyes were turned on the boy. He suddenly came out of his dream and looked straight at his master.

"But master," he cried in desperate appeal, "I didn't take it."

"Nonsense," shouted the goldsmith, suddenly wriggling himself the right way up like a caterpillar. "Nonsense. Lies!"

Philemon took no notice. He gazed steadily at the boy.

"Then how did it get there?" he asked rather sadly.

How had it got there? Onesimus, in his shock and fear, had not yet asked that question. He had thought of nothing but the branding. But the question must be answered. He stared at Philemon open-mouthed and then, suddenly, he turned and stared at Archippus.

But their eyes met only for a moment. The older boy

flushed crimson and turned away. There was a long silence, broken only by the chattering of the goldsmith; and Philemon looked first at his son and then at his slave, and the blood seemed to thunder in Onesimus' head till he thought it would burst.

"Gold cannot disappear without hands," said Philemon at last, "and you knew the price. Take him away, Janus, and do it quickly."

Archippus suddenly stepped forward. He did not look at Onesimus, but stood in front of his father, hands clasped, pleading.

"Father, father," he cried, "not branding. He's only young. Father, pardon him. Let him be beaten with rods, but not branding!"

His father hesitated. Archippus, spurning the old man out of his way with his foot, fell on his knees before Philemon.

"Oh, father, have mercy..."

A soft voice at his side made Philemon turn. His beautiful wife, Apphia, had laid her hand on his arm and spoke timidly, for it was not her place to enter into judgment.

"My husband, he is your slave who serves you in front of our guests. Do you want him spoiled and disfigured? As our son says, he is young. Let the rods teach him. If it happens again, he will be branded."

Philemon smiled at her. He never could refuse her anything, and her gentle wishes were the law of the home. He turned back to Onesimus and spoke sternly.

"You are fortunate! Render thanks to the gods for a merciful mistress, and take heed to yourself in the future. Now, go with Janus and be taught by the rods.

Silence, Master Goldsmith, and be gone! You shall be given a gold piece to make up for the trouble my slave has caused you."

Twenty minutes later, Onesimus, faint and sick, dragged himself to his hut, and his mother asked no questions, for she had been a slave all her life, and this was the natural lot of the slave. But she drew his mat to the doorway because the hut was warm and airless and she knew her son would be feverish before nightfall. Then she washed his wounds and anointed them with oil and brought him fresh, cool water from the spring. He lay quite still till dusk, his face resting on his arms, too sore and stiff to move, but his brain worked furiously.

Yes, how did it get there? He had put two and two together now, and he knew. When, oh when would he be free to work out his revenge? The strength of his hatred and the impotence of his hatred nearly drove him mad. He was a slave, and there was nothing whatever that he could do but lie there and hate, and hate, and hate.

"Mother," he called, turning his head with difficulty, "how much money is there in the clay money-box hidden under the hearth-stone?"

"Only your gold half-aureus, and a few copper and brass coins," answered his mother gently; "but it will come. Have patience, my son. Do not be like your father who fretted his life away in rebellion against his lot. The gods know best."

Stealthy footsteps were heard on the mud path, and Archippus crept round the corner of the hut with a cup in his hand, a cup containing a mixture of diluted wine, myrrh and oil. When he spoke, his voice was unsteady and pleading.

"I have brought you some posca for your wounds," he said, "And - and - I'm glad you were not branded."

Onesimus took the cup, flung it on the ground with all the strength he could muster and spat. Archippus fled, and Onesimus felt better. To give vent to his hatred was a more powerful tonic than posca. Tomorrow Archippus would go to Laodicea, and he need not set eyes on him all day. After that... well, it was better to live a day at a time.

He was glad that he would be too stiff and lame to accompany his master to Laodicea. He did not want Eirene to see him servile and obedient, standing in the background, ordered about by Archippus. Let her keep the memory of that day when they were both free children together, swinging their legs above the deep pool in the canyon and laughing. The thought of her somehow eased his misery, and he fell into a restless sleep and dreamed that they were once again back in the canyon, but that she was running ahead, beckoning him to follow. The cascade was roaring, but the grass between the rocks was soft to the feet, and spring flowers seemed to bloom in her tracks. And he knew she was going up and up on swift tireless feet to the hidden lakes and the snowy summits, to freedom and beauty and life, and he was free to follow.

And then, he awoke to pain and darkness and fever and cried out for his mother.

Next day he dragged himself out on to the hillside and sat resting till the sun was high in the sky, warming a little of the stiffness out of him. He watch the procession set out for Laodicea across the upper plain and disappear over the first descent into the valley. Archippus and

Philemon were mounted on beautiful steeds, wearing coloured coats made in the best style in the Laodicean factories. A small retinue of slaves followed, mounted on humbler beasts, and Onesimus followed them in his imagination. They would jolt downhill to the lower plain which was green, warm and luxuriant and sheltered from the snow and winds that roared across the plain above. Then the valley would be directly beneath them, and they would jog down the stony tracks, between the bare vineyards and silver olive groves, to join the Eastern highway in the valley.

The Eastern highway! The very words thrilled him, for four great roads converged on Laodicea, and the traveller could turn where he would, and the world lay before him. Often in his imagination Onesimus travelled on those roads: north-west to Philadelphia and to Sardis, the wealthy luxurious city with its gold-bearing river running through its very market-place; north-east to the Phrygian plains, the Taurus mountains, the Cilician Gates, and on to the lands of spices and ivory; south to Perga where the mountains rolled down to the coast; west to the great sea-port of Ephesus, the blue Aegean sea, the islands, the land of his father, the mountains of the gods. He lay there dozing till afternoon, letting the spring sunshine warm and heal him. Then he was jerked suddenly back from his happy dreams, for a man was climbing the hill that led to their home.

He was not old, but he seemed tired, and he leaned on his staff. He was not a particularly fine looking man, but there was something about him that attracted the boy's attention. Perhaps it was the quiet strength of his lean face or the clearness of his eyes. He was dressed simply, and when he came near to Onesimus he spoke in the local Phrygian dialect.

"Grace and peace be to you, my son," said the man, "Is this the farm of Philemon, and is he at home?"

"It is his house," replied Onesimus, "but he is not there. He has ridden into Laodicea on business, and he will probably not be back till sundown."

"Then tell him his old friend, Master Epaphras, called on him," said the man." "He will remember, for we grew up here together as boys. Tell him I am staying at my old home, and I will call again."

"Yes, master," replied Onesimus; but the man did not move. He stood feasting his eyes on the rugged valley, already softened by the green of spring. His eyes swept the landscape: the winding river valley, the proud little hill on which stood Laodicea, and the rocky fortress of Hierapolis with its white glacier of limestone.

"It is a beautiful land," he said suddenly. "I should like to sit and rest for a few moments, for I have been walking since sunrise. And if you could bring me a cup of cold water I should thank you exceedingly."

Onesimus rose stiffly and painfully to his feet and hobbled to his hut. His mother was up at the house helping Mistress Apphia; but he fetched fresh water and a platter of olives, dates and dried figs, arranging them with care and a little fear. Had not Zeus and Hermes visited old Philemon and Baucis at Lystra to the East, and had they not greatly rewarded them for their hospitality. These things happened, and you could never be sure. There was a light on this man's face that made him different from other men.

"You are in pain, my son," said the man gently as

Onesimus returned and stood respectfully beside him. "Sit on the grass beside me and tell me what happened."

Onesimus got into a comfortable position and scowled.

"I am a slave, Master," he said, "and yesterday I was beaten with rods for a crime I had not committed."

"That is hard," said Epaphras, "but it has happened before. It happened to Jesus Christ. They crucified Him for crimes He never committed. He prayed for their forgiveness."

Onesimus started angrily. Jesus Christ again! Was that name always to pursue and haunt him? This crucified vanquished weakling! But he controlled his annoyance and answered politely.

"Well, Master, it did not do him much good, did it, if they crucified him? It would have been better to have resisted. I mean, they conquered him in the end."

"And now, at the right hand of God exalted, He is conquering thousands by His love. Love is stronger than death and stronger than hatred. It conquers all in the end. It has conquered me."

"But I do not want to be conquered," persisted the boy. "All my life I have been a slave, but one day I shall buy my freedom. I want to be free to go where I wish and to do as I please and to revenge wrong. I hate this bondage, and I hate those who accuse me falsely and punish me without cause."

"But Jesus Christ can set you free today," replied the man, and his voice rang with triumph. "He can free you from your discontent and your hatred. Tell me, does your hatred make you happy?"

The boy was about to answer, and then hesitated.

He suddenly remembered how in the night he had wept out his hatred into his pillow and cursed the darkness, and how he had thought that the dawn would never come. He remembered, too, the peace in his mother's eyes when she had risen up to bathe his wounds and to give him a drink. He stared moodily into space, and then his eyes rested on the proud city across the valley, and he remembered again the afternoon when a little run-away Laodicean maid had taken his heart captive. Dimly he realised, for the first time, that there were other ways of conquering besides hatred and strife. The answer died on his lips.

5

IF THIS TEACHING BRINGS A SURE HOPE OF eternal life and joy, then let us take heed to it." It was Apphia who spoke, her hand on her husband's knee, her face lifted to his. Epaphras had visited his old boyhood friend in the morning, and they had been delighted to see each other, and Philemon had ordered a sumptuous midday meal. But the food had grown cold and lain almost untouched on the platters as Epaphras revealed the real purpose of his visit. Far into the afternoon he and Philemon had talked and argued, and Archippus had sat listening, clasping his knees, sullen and silent. And in the shadows of her room, Apphia, too, sat listening, unnoticed, for this was men's talk, and nobody supposed that she was paying any attention.

And now the guest was gone and the all but untasted food had been removed. Archippus had gone to his duties, and Philemon and Apphia were left alone. Then, in the quiet of the evening hour, she had come forward and sat down on a low stool at her husband's feet.

"How have I feared death!" cried Apphia. "Often in winter, when the goddess mother mourns her daughter who has returned to the underworld, and the wind moans in the rocks and the jackals howl in the canyons and the nights are long and dark, I have thought, 'Is this what death will be like, to go out into the winter gloom of the underworld where demons howl?' Our dead go in through the doorways of our Phyrgian graves, but who has ever come back to tell us how they fare, except this Christ?"

"But, my love," murmured Philemon, deeply moved in spite of himself, "a crucified Jew, a Galilean peasant, put to death by the Romans! It is fantastic."

Little Pascasia wandered into the room, and her father lifted her on to his knee.

"But He conquered death," insisted Apphia, "and He endured that crucifixion of His own free will. No one conquered Him. Have you forgotten what Master Epaphras said? His death was an act of love and atoning sacrifice. Have any of our gods loved like that? Artemis, the huntress, pursues to destroy, and Zeus in his paradise hurls thunderbolts at us; and we fear the demons who haunt the rocks and the gods who pay no heed. Do they come to us, as He comes, and say, 'Fear not,' or 'I am the way'?"

"Hush," said Philemon, thoroughly alarmed. "Do you not fear the vengeance of the gods, that you dare to talk like that?"

"If gods there be, up there in the clouds," replied Apphia boldly. "He spoke of one God who came down to us and had compassion on us and suffered for us; and my heart tells me that this is the true God. Tonight, I shall pray to Him; and oh, my husband, I entreat you to pray with me, as Master Epaphras taught us to do!"

Philemon sat in silence for a long time. A soft-footed slave came in to light the lamps, but his master motioned him away, and the room grew dark, and up above the vine trellises the stars shone down on them. Then the moon rose behind the mountains, flooding the little courtyard with silver light.

"But we should lose our trade and our contracts," he said at last. "Men have been stoned and killed and crucified because they have followed this Christ. That Paul, of whom Epaphras was speaking, was nearly lynched two or three times in Galatia and beaten up and imprisoned in Macedonia. Have you counted the cost, Apphia?"

"Glory and eternal life," she replied instantly. "Other men have endured, and so can we. Paul is preaching the news in Ephesus, and they say it is spreading like a summer fire! There are believers in Hierapolis, in Laodicea, in Smyrna and in Philadelphia. They say there are a few names even in Sardis. The fire of the love of this Christ is spreading, my husband, and one day I believe it will blaze out through the whole world."

"Listen," said Philemon, torn between, doubt and fear. "I will do this. Yesterday, Master Polemon urged me to go and visit his friends at the seaport of Ephesus and to try and join the guild. They export wool, and Polemon has mentioned me as an honest merchant. I had already purposed to go at the time of the Artemisia and to take Archippus with me. I can do my business, and he would enjoy the games and the processions. The boy Onesimus can go with him to attend on him, and that will leave me free. Then I will visit this Paul myself and hear with my own ears what he has to say. I shall not stay long, for it will be the time of the sheep shearing, but the older slaves are trustworthy enough, and you can keep watch over things in my absence."

So Apphia kissed her husband and took Pascasia to bed. Philemon sat for a long time, thinking. But Archippus lay tossing on his mattress, too restless to sleep. The crime he had committed weighed heavily on his conscience, and today Master Epaphras had spoken much of sin and judgment. He had also spoken of repentance and forgiveness; but repentance meant confession, and that was too hard a condition for proud young Archippus. So he slept and woke and tossed, and slept again and woke again and hated the dark, till at last the cock crew, and he was glad because the dawn would soon steal in his little window, and with the coming of a new day he might forget. He would go and tell Onesimus that they were going to the Artemisia, and maybe, in his delight Onesimus would forget too.

The Artemisia took place in the month of May, and it was already April, so there was much ado to get ready. Onesimus, who was strong as a young ox, recovered quickly from his beating and was inwardly full of excited anticipation, although in front of Archippus he remained stonily obedient and showed no pleasure at all.

The great day dawned at last, and the procession set out at daybreak. The cisium, a light, open, two-wheeled carriage drawn by a horse, was waiting at the gate on Philemon, with a senior slave as driver. Archippus, mounted on a fine steed, stood ready to ride beside his father. Onesimus and one other attendant were to ride behind on fast mules with the luggage.

Philemon appeared at last with Apphia beside him and his daughter in his arms. His wife seemed to have been pleading with him, for he loosened her hold of him gently and kissed her hand and murmured, "Peace be with you, dear one. I will not forget, and I will tell you all." Then he handed her the clinging child and climbed into the carriage. The slave gave rein to the impatient beast and they were off at a good pace.

Late April on the upper plains! It was the very high-tide of Spring and the asphodels and irises followed the rushing of the streams. Fat lambs pranced in meadows of marigold and pink mallow, and the cries of the newly-shorn sheep filled the warm air. As they dipped toward the valley, Onesimus noticed new fig leaves, like small rabbits' ears, bursting from the ashen grey wood. Truly the earth was very good, and he wanted no other gods and goddesses than the Mother of Nature who scattered the Spring over the waiting land, and the Sun god who rode his chariot across the heavens and warmed and cheered him, and Aphrodite, the goddess of beauty who cried to his heart in the asphodels and the young green wheat and the white clouds and the shimmering mountains behind Hierapolis. Yes, today the earth was all good, and he had forgotten his slavery.

The jolting track down through the olive groves broadened out, and the hooves of their beasts clattered on the Eastern highway, and Onesimus' heart thrilled as they joined the crowd of vehicles and pilgrims travelling west to the Artemisia. They were streaming in from every region in Asia as north, south, east and west converged: from Pamphylia, Phrygia, Galatia, Bithynia, and perhaps much further, for the Eastern highway ran as far as the great river, the river Euphrates.

And now they were at the place where two rivers met. The Lycus glen had broadened out into the fertile valley of the Meander. Now they were clattering gaily along beneath the very walls of Laodicea which stood on a small hillock a hundred and fifty feet or so above the valley. Its fortifications looked impregnable, but its Syrian gate was open, and travellers streamed forth to join the pilgrimage.

"One day I shall walk through that gate a free man," said Onesimus to himself and fell a-dreaming of beauty and freedom. Was little Mistress Eirene out in the meadows this morning, gathering irises and asphodels? One day they would gather flowers together. Anything was possible today, for he was young and strong and happy, and it was springtime.

It was a full hundred miles from Laodicea to Ephesus, and it was impossible to hurry; for as they travelled westwards the highway became more and more thronged with carriages, litters, ox-carts, gigs mules and horses, all going the same way. On the second day, the express courier from Rome, drawn by fast horses fresh from the last Government house, came thundering down the highway, the driver blowing his horn to warn everyone to get out of the way. Beasts shied, pilgrims on foot screamed, and a light cisium was overturned as the horse swerved to the side of the road. But Onesimus paid no attention to the injured occupants. He was staring after that swaying chariot and the galloping horses. These men had come all the way from Rome, from the very presence of Nero, the glorious, new god-like Emperor. One day he would go to Rome.

The inns along the road were over-flowing, and Philemon and Archippus grumbled freely at the dirty overcrowded accommodation and the cursing, squabbling hordes of travellers who kept them awake all night. Onesimus and the other slaves fared better; for they slept out with the beasts under the stars, and in this southern valley the spring nights were warm and the air was sweet. He enjoyed every moment of the crowded journey, with its jostling and fighting and joking, and at midday, when they had prepared food and his master was resting, he and Archippus would wade through the rushes and bathe in the river.

At Antioch on the Meander they crossed the beautiful six-arched bridge over the river and took the northern fork of the road to Ephesus. They were not far from the coast now, and the mountains on either side of the valley broadened out into a fertile plain. Rocks, cedars and cypresses gave way to young wheat and bean fields and orchards of fig trees. It was a warm, sleepy, scented country, the tired pilgrims turned in early that night; for tomorrow, on the morning of the fourth day, they would reach Ephesus.

Onesimus was up long before daybreak and had groomed and saddled the horses and swept out the chariot before the other slaves had opened their eyes. He was desperately excited, for today he would look on the city of his dreams. His master would rest on arrival, and in the evening of that very day they would visit the temple of Artemis, or Diana as the Greeks called her, the glorious mother of life and fertility. Tonight he would see her of whom men spoke with bated breath. What did he expect to see? He did not know; but surely tonight he would see perfect beauty, the very source from which flowed all the life and beauty he had ever known, or knew at that moment: the flowers at his feet, the dawn breaking over the eastward mountains behind him, the soft smell of the spring, and the face of a child. Tonight he would know and understand.

6

NEVER WOULD ONESIMUS FORGET HIS FIRST sight of Ephesus, the supreme metropolis of Asia, as they rounded a bend in the hills and saw the city spread out before them, its marble pillars and temples dazzling in the morning sunlight, the waters of the harbour sparkling, and the sea beyond the canal peacock blue. The encircling heights of Mount Coressus sloped down to the Aegean, and the city lay as though cradled to the south-west in a green protecting arm. Even the most hardened pilgrims paused and held their breath and worshipped, for here was beauty incarnate, the fitting home and shrine of the fair goddess whose temple even now lay in full view on the low-lying ground north of the city, one of the seven great wonders of the world. It was built facing the harbour so that every tired sailor whose ship entered the canal could lift up his eyes and view it from afar and be blessed and strengthened by the bounty of the goddess.

Onesimus stood as though rooted to the spot, until the older slave dug him sharply in the ribs with his riding whip. Philemon and Archippus were already pushing ahead, expecting their slaves to follow close behind them, and it was not easy to keep together in the excited sweating throng. The boy had never in his life seen so many people, and said so.

His fellow slave laughed. "There are yet five days to the Artemisia," he said. "It will be a lot worse yet. Thank the gods you came early."

Polemon had already arranged for a comfortable apartment for his merchant friend and sent his own slave to prepare it. It was a relief to turn in from the blazing streets to the cool shaded atrium and to find a bath and a meal and beds ready and stables for the horses. Onesimus was sent off immediately to care for the weary beasts, and, his work done, he lingered long at the gate, gazing up at the exquisite temples and the great theatre on the hill that dominated the town. There were twenty-four thousand seats in that theatre, and no doubt he would go in attendance on Archippus and see the Pan-Ionian games. He was tempted to run out across the harbour street and peep at the Agora, or market place, that lay beyond; but he was recalled by an angry voice.

"Whatever are you doing, idle slave? You could have stabled a legion of horses by this time. Our masters have bathed and robed and are about to eat. You should be in attendance on them."

Philemon and Archippus were both hungry and very tired. They had slept badly in the inns for three nights past, and the heat of the low-lying sheltered city was stifling. They ate well but said little, and when they had finished Philemon pointed at the remains of the meal.

"My son and I will retire to rest," he said to the slaves. "Eat of what is left, and prepare another bath, and attend to our travelling clothes, and get ready the evening meal. When we have slept and the day is a little cooler, we will proceed to the temple on foot, and you shall wait on us. I hear that the temple is a sanctuary for murderers, thieves and pickpockets, and you will need to guard our persons most diligently. We will eat on our return."

The older slave, whose name was Hermes, went off to shop for their supper, and Onesimus ate hastily and worked hard for there was much to do and he had already offended by staying so long in the stables. He, too, was worn out with the early start, the excitement and the heat and could hardly keep his eyes open. He glanced in at Archippus, snoring in his luxurious apartment, and once again hate surged up in his heart. One day he would harm this boy, defeat him, spoil his life. But the time was not yet. He must be patient, always patient. Tonight he would see the fair goddess and pray for blessing and success.

It was late afternoon when the two awoke and bathed and dressed with great care for their visit to the temple which lay nearly a mile from the city. It was cooler now, and they were grateful for it; for the crowds were denser than ever. Tonight the great goddess would be unveiled to the worshipping throng, and her devotees and priests were doing their best to work the crowd into a frenzy. All along the street, between the fluted marble pillars, were booths filled with strange silvery images, some very large, some small enough to be worn as charms, and between them sat the writers of the famous Ephesian letters - scrolls of words which none could understand but which were believed to be the most powerful spells and charms. To carry one in your bosom was to carry a talisman against evil and a guarantee of success. Everyone in Ephesus knew the story of the Greek wrestler in the Olympic games who threw every opponent until it was discovered that he was wearing an Ephesian letter tied to his ankle, and when that was removed he became as weak as any other man.

Yet there was a strange restlessness in the air and a sense of battle. Why did silversmiths advertise their goods so frantically and the writers of magic so entreat people to buy, affirming over and over again the sovereignty of Artemis? Was her sovereignty threatened? Once or twice they overheard quiet scraps of conversation in the streets.

"It will not be as last year... The goddess is no longer supreme... Have men been healed in the name of Artemis? There are almost as many gathering at the school of Tyrannus... There are sure to be riots, Jews and Asians... They turned him out of the synagogue two years ago..."

Onesimus pricked up his ears. It sounded interesting. A riot in this place would be wonderful, but what would they riot about, and why were men gathering in a school? He glanced at Philemon, but his master's face was sombre and thoughtful. Not far from the temple he stopped at the shop of Demetrius, the largest and most fashionable of the silversmiths, and examined the beautiful models for sale. He bought an expensive image, the size of his fist, and a tiny charm on a silver chain.

"For your mother and Pascasia," he said to his son. "They will like them." He put them carefully in his wallet and moved on to the next booth where a magician sat, surrounded by books of magic, writing busily. Philemon hesitated, watched him for a moment, and then bought two of the finest letters.

"I shall need them tomorrow," he said to Archippus. "I have to see Master Polemon's friend the wool merchant down at the harbour about joining the guild. It will greatly increase our fortunes if I am accepted."

Demetrius' shop was close to the temple, and with a little shiver of fear and hope and wonder Onesimus followed his master into the precincts. He was to wait with Hermes near the door while Philemon and Archippus pushed their way forward towards the altar and the inner shrine; but even at the back Onesimus could see enough to thrill him. It was nearly sunset, and here indeed was perfect beauty. The evening light streamed down between the hundred and twenty-seven pillars of the colonnades so that the rich reds and golds and blues shone with an unearthly brightness, each pillar the gift of a king. But the centre of the temple was roofed with cedar, dimly lighted by lamps, and the air was heavy with incense and the smell of sweating humanity.

At first Onesimus only looked at the pillars and the glowing colours, at the great staircase cut from one gigantic vine from Cyprus, at the famous old altar and the draped curtains, at the beauty of the last light. But the light was fading now, and he began to be aware of what was happening in the dark. He looked at the faces of the men who lounged near him at the entrance of the Temple, and he felt afraid, for they were evil sin-seared faces, the faces of criminals and murderers, clinging to their sanctuary. He edged further into the darkness to be nearer to the worshippers, and then he felt still more afraid. Something was happening he could not understand. The quiet mutterings had grown to a kind of hysterical screaming and the whole crowd was becoming frenzied. The curtain was being drawn up, inch by inch, and in another moment her glory would shine on him, and he would forget the cut-throats and the rogues and the sickening smell. Cool beauty and light would flow to him, and it would be Spring in his soul.

And then, as the curtain lifted further, the insane shrieking grew louder, and he saw her over the heads of the swaying multitude - a hideous squat idol, a repulsive caricature of a woman, carved from old black wood, ending in a rough stump, nobbled, and holding in her hands a club and a trident. An eerie light shone down on her which made the darkness around him seem deeper. And suddenly he was aware of evil things happening under cover of darkness. The incense-laden air was thick with evil. A hand took hold of him; but he screamed and broke loose and fought his way out into the open air.

Sick and faint, he made for the strip of marshland that lay between the temple and the sea, and, flinging himself down, pressed his forehead to the cool grass. Light still lingered in the western sky above the harbour, a rosy light reflected in the water. Yes, there was still beauty in the world, but it was as far removed from the goddess as light from darkness, as life from death. He felt more afraid than he had ever felt before. He thought of the rock tombs that they had passed along the highway, shaped like doorways. Was this death? To pass through those doors into the stifling darkness, to draw near to *Her*? Yet surely his father's gods had not been like that? One day he would go to Greece and climb the flowery slopes of Parnassus and seek for his father's gods.

He dared not stay long in the marsh, for he had been ordered to wait by the door of the temple to escort his master home. Hermes was standing just where he had left him, awed by the worship, but not greatly moved, for he was of Phrygian peasant stock, as solid as his own Taurus mountains. Onesimus stood as far away as he dared, and he shivered, for the twilight was cool and fresh after the stifling atmosphere of the temple, and the worship was only just beginning. The crowd would sway and shriek and chant till dawn, and many would fall down in a swoon, and some would die. It might be hours before Philemon and Archippus appeared.

But they did not have to wait long. The sickle moon was just visible over the crest of Mount Prion when Philemon pushed his way out, half-carrying his son who had fainted. He revived in the cold air, but his face was chalky white and there was a haunted look in his eyes.

"Home," said Philemon briefly. They walked back to their apartment in silence and Archippus went straight to his bed. But Philemon ordered wine, dismissed his slaves and stayed drinking far into the night. Twice Onesimus woke and lay on his pallet of straw listening to his master's footsteps pacing up and down, up and down, on the paved atrium. At dawn he was still pacing to and fro under the paling stars.

At breakfast Archippus had recovered and was eager to see the sights, but Philemon was heavy-eyed and moody. He drank his wine in silence and then gave orders for the day. "Hermes, order a litter, and I and my son will drive to the harbour now and discuss my business, while Onesimus sets the house in order. We shall return before noon, and Onesimus will accompany us on foot to the school of Tyrannus."

"Why father?" asked Archippus.

"To listen to a discourse by a man named Paul of Tarsus," answered his father shortly. "He holds forth daily as soon as the scholars leave for their midday meal and goes on till the ninth hour when they return. I hear that the school is crowded all through the siesta hour. They say he has many disciples."

Onesimus, left alone, set the house in order and fed the horses, laid out clean clothes for his master, prepared the light midday meal and then sat down in the doorway to watch the throngs of people walking up and down the harbour street between the fluted marble pillars: companies of gay ladies going up to the ladies' baths, magnificent young gladiators on their way to the gymnasium, shoppers bound for the Agora jostling against swarthy Egyptian sailors strolling back to their ships. At one point the people made way as a proud Roman governor was carried up to the town hall in a handsome litter with the magistrates and town clerk riding behind him in procession. Onesimus could have stayed there all day watching. But his fun was short-lived, for Philemon and Archippus returned in a surprisingly short time, and they set out together for the school of Tyrannus.

The school lay half way up the hill, and Onesimus longed to linger and look. There was so much to see: the colourful Agora, the world-famous library, buildings and monuments whose strength and beauty would defy time, and whose immortal carvings would still amaze the world after two thousand years. But there was no time to stand and stare that morning, for Philemon and Archippus walked fast. There were many going the same way, and Onesimus had difficulty in keeping them in sight. The going was the more difficult on account of the merry little scholars, just out of school, who were all

Patricia St. John

pushing in the opposite direction.

They had arrived; for the crowd had turned into a side street and were streaming through the door of a large hall, the school of Master Tyrannus. It was a big crowd, but it was different from any other crowd Onesimus had ever met, for no one pushed or jostled or fought for the front seats.

The people entered with grave dignity, making way for the weak or the old, and a sense of quiet expectancy hung over the room. Onesimus looked round in amazement from his slave's position at the door, rubbed his eyes to make sure he was not dreaming, and then looked again.

Half the congregation were Jews, and yet there was no middle wall of partition down the centre of the hall. They all sat together in apparent harmony, Jew and Gentile, men and women, black and white, Roman, Greek and Macedonian, rich and poor, slave and free. A deep silence now brooded over the room and many appeared to be worshipping. Then a man climbed on to the master's dais and every eye was turned upon him as he began to speak.

He was a small, insignificant looking Jew, with strange scars on his face and burning eyes that seemed to be looking far beyond the rapt multitude at his feet. What had he seen, wondered Onesimus with a little shiver, and what had he got to say? And anyhow, what were they all doing in this stifling hall, listening to this strange little Jew, when they might have been up at the theatre stage watching the gladiators?

"Grace and peace!" cried Paul, beckoning to a couple of slaves who stood hesitating in the doorway. "Jesus

Christ has made peace by the blood of His Cross. You that were near, and you that were far, Christ is our peace. He has broken down the middle wall of partition, and now there is no longer Jew or Greek, male or female, bond or free. We are all one in Christ Jesus."

Jesus Christ! It was the same name, challenging him at every turn. The boy at the door hung his head, for the little man on the dais seemed now to be looking straight at him. "Peace, through the blood of His Cross. He is our peace, Jesus Christ suffering, submitting, accepting and forgiving."

But Onesimus did not want peace at that price. He wanted to rise and rebel and to live as he pleased and to fight for his freedom and to work out his revenge. He slipped behind a pillar, sat down and blocked his ears.

7

THE HOT CROWDED DAYS ROLLED PAST AND the Artemisia was upon them. It was the day when the statue of Artemis would be carried through the streets of the city on a car drawn by fawns, right from the temple in the marshes to the arena on Mount Prion, and the great athletic contests of the Artemisia would start. The boys had waked at dawn to the sound of flutes and trumpets, the shouting of the heralds and the thundering of the sculptured drums. No business would be done today. They waited impatiently for Philemon to appear and give orders.

He was not in his bedroom, and they found him on the roof, gazing pre-occupied out to sea. He looked weary and old, and there were dark circles under his eyes. When he turned to the eager lads, dressed in their best clothes, his look was troubled.

"Oh," he said, addressing his son and handing him a small wallet, "the slaves will attend upon you, and here is money to enter the games and to buy refreshment. I am not going today. I am going back to the school of Tyrannus."

"Father!" Archippus' voice broke in disappointment. "You are not coming to the first great day of the games? Surely no one will go and listen to Master Paul today. It is the day of the great procession and sacrifice. Have you forgotten?"

Philemon smiled. "No, I have not forgotten," he said gently, "but I cannot come. Perhaps I have no more part in these processions and sacrifices. There is another altar, but I don't know yet. I only know that today I must go and listen again."

Archippus stood very still, gazing at his father whom he loved and admired deeply. It was the first time any rift had ever come between them. They had been completely one on their aim of building a happy luxurious home and prospering in business. But during the past two or three days Philemon had seemed to care little for business and had said nothing about his interview with the merchants.

"Father," the boy pleaded suddenly, "this teaching is going to spoil our life. What guild will receive a Christian? Everyone is talking about them. They are despised heretics. How shall we live?"

"We should live for the eternal, for the things not seen," said Philemon simply. "But, my son, I do not know yet. If it is true that we can be filled with the very life of the One Everlasting God here on earth, then what is wealth or business or anything else compared with that? But how to know whether this is true? I must hear more and learn more, and I have neither time nor heart to attend to these processions. Was there truth or goodness or purity in the temple that night?"

Archippus grew pale with fear and glanced round to see if the slaves had heard. But they were waiting below and his father had spoken softly. It was the first time they had brought up the subject of the visit to the temple, and Archippus dared not give voice to his thoughts. He clasped his hands uneasily.

"Today," he said, "I will go and see the games and the processions. Tomorrow, father, I will come with you to the school of Tyrannus."

The boys and Hermes returned at sunset, well pleased with all they had seen, but tired out with the heat and noise and crowds. The festivities would go on far into the night, the religious fervour increasing in frenzy. Onesimus would gladly have stayed, but Archippus had ordered them home, for he was suffering from mild sunstroke and felt sick and feverish. He had been irritable all day and unusually rude to his slaves. Onesimus could gladly have kicked him down the harbour street.

Philemon was sitting waiting at the atrium and had already eaten. He rose up at once and helped his son to bed and took him wine and a sleeping draught. Then he turned to the slaves.

"Hermes," he said, "stay and attend to your young master. Onesimus, I am going to pay a call, and you will come with me."

Onesimus set off behind his master in a thoroughly bad temper. He had had no supper and drunk no wine and he, too, was feeling sick and giddy with heat. Where on earth was his master going? The district round the harbour was almost deserted, for everyone was up on the hill in the precincts of the theatre. They had reached the poorer quarter of the town, and still Philemon hurried on through the badly lit streets, unsure now of his bearings, hesitating at the turnings.

A woman stood in a doorway with a baby in her arms. Philemon addressed her.

"Can you direct me to the house of Paul the tent-maker?" he asked.

She nodded, as though quite used to this request, and pointed to a lighted cottage just opposite. The doorway was low and Philemon had to stoop to enter. Onesimus followed, scornful and amazed. He was still more amazed at the scene that met his eyes. It was all he could do to stop himself from bursting out laughing.

Paul the venerable, Paul the honoured teacher of a new religion, Paul whose name was becoming famous throughout Asia, the learned Jew of Tarsus, was sitting on the floor with his legs in a pit weaving black goats-hair into an upright loom. On a stool beside him lay a finished scroll, a letter he had been writing. Cross-legged round him sat his friends, talking earnestly above the whine of the shuttle and the clack of the loom. Their faces, pale in the lamplight, were grave, and none of them noticed the new arrival.

"I have told them," cried Paul, waving his hand toward the scroll and addressing four cultured scholarly Corinthians who sat close to him and who looked thoroughly out of place in the weaving shed, "I have told them in no uncertain language that not many wise, not many mighty, not many noble are called, that no flesh should glory in God's presence. Indeed, I have poured out my heart to them. Oh, Achaicus and Stephanas, my sons in Christ, go back and teach them that not by wisdom or learning can a man know God or the deep things of God, but by repentance, faith, holiness and love. Bid them to cease this party strife and to cast out the sin in their midst and to build on one foundation."

"But Master," said a third man anxiously, "what about the questions they asked about church discipline and order? They need to know the answers."

"I have answered all, Fortunatus," replied Paul, again indicating the letter; "but it is all to no avail unless they have repented. Though they understand all mysteries and all knowledge but have not love, they are nothing. Tell them to follow after love and then the Spirit will teach them all. Oh, my brothers, the churches in Galatia fell through false doctrine. God forbid, the church in Corinth should fall through pride and strife and uncleanness."

"Brother Paul, there is a new arrival ." A voice spoke from the back of the room, where another craftsman was feeding the goats-hair into the loom for the tent cloth. His features were unmistakably Jewish. He moved forward into the light and drew Philemon in.

"Welcome to my humble home," he said, "and let the boy come in too." Then seeing Philemon's amazement at being welcomed into a Jewish house, he smiled. "There are no barriers here," he said gently. "Christ has died for all. Peace be unto you. On what errand do you come?"

All eyes were turned on the handsome Phrygian who stood in the shadow of the doorway, and he answered humbly, "I seek for truth. I want to know and worship the true and living God."

The circle in the lamplight moved up and made room for him and he sat down near the loom. Onesimus crept to the back where a small boy held the yarn, and Aquila the weaver joined them and went quietly on with his work. He was a poor man and could not afford to lose time.

"You shall find what you seek," said the apostle. "God has revealed Himself. His light has shined upon our darkness. All of us within this room have seen it. The glory of God has been revealed in the face of Jesus Christ."

His voice in the weaving shed sounded like a trumpet proclaiming some tremendous dawn. Once again Onesimus shivered. What had they seen, this company of men with their lifted rapt faces? What had Stephen seen? He no longer wanted to laugh. He felt almost as afraid as he had felt in the temple of Artemis, but it was a different kind of fear. There it was fear of evil; here it was fear of something else, something before which evil must shrivel up. Then the door at the other end of the weaving shed was opened, and a woman with a gentle face looked in. "Come, Levi," she said softly, beckoning to the little boy. "It is time you supped and slept."

The child rose at once and ran to his mother, but not before she had caught sight of the weary child slumped against the wall, and she guessed that he must be the slave of the distinguished newcomer. Recently exiled from Rome with her Jewish husband, Priscilla had seen enough of slavery in her native capital to make her hate the whole system, and she beckoned Onesimus to follow little Levi into the living room behind the weaving shed.

"Have you supped?" she asked smiling. "These men, once they start talking, may go on all night. You had better eat this and lie down and sleep. My husband will call you when your master is ready."

He drank the buttermilk and ate the barley bread and goat's cheese, which she gave him, very gratefully and flung himself down on a pile of skins and was soundly asleep within a moment... and then, someone was shaking him gently, and he started up in a fright. Surely, he had only just lain down? Then he saw a grey light stealing in from the courtyard and he knew that it was early morning.

He was reeling and confused with sleep. Where was he, and what had happened? Priscilla, laughing a little, brought cold water to bathe his face, and her hands were kind, like his own mother's. He mumbled his thanks and staggered into the weaving shed and stole a scared glance at his master, and that glance woke him up completely. He knew now what had happened. Philemon, too, had seen.

There was no one in the room except Paul and Philemon. All the others had long since gone home; but it takes time to bring a man's whole life into the light of God, and the tired apostle looked as though he had fought some great battle and conquered. Philemon suddenly dropped at his feet, and Paul raised his hands over him and blessed him.

"The Lord bless thee and keep thee, my son in Christ. The Lord make his face to shine upon thee, and bring thee to His eternal glory through Jesus Christ our Lord." And then, somehow, they were out in the grey deserted streets and Philemon drew his cloak round him, for an east wind was blowing down from Mount Prion.

They turned the corner into the harbour street and looked seaward through the frame of marble pillars, and both caught their breath. All the sunrise was reflected in the still waters of the harbour, and the sea beyond the canal was a line of silver. A corn ship, caught in the dawn wind, had started for the open sea, heeling over leeward, her sails billowing, light as the wings of a bird as they caught the first rays.

"His light hath shined in our darkness," murmured Philemon, and he stood for a full five minutes watching the beautiful craft setting out so gallantly towards the bright open sea and the lands where the sun sets. The storms would come, but the beginning was always glorious. Warmed by the glow of his great joy, he quite forgot his shivering young slave who had no cloak.

Then he turned and saw him, and a strange compassion he had never known before welled within him. He suddenly remembered that Onesimus had left the house without supper, and all through that glorious, never-to-be-forgotten night he had certainly never given a thought as to how or where the boy was sleeping. Why should he? The master's comfort was the business of the slave, but the slave's comfort was not the affair of his master.

But now? Something had happened. He seemed to be seeing the whole world with eyes that had been opened. The colours of the sky were fairer, the scent of the acacia more poignant, and the coldness and weariness of the boy at his side suddenly mattered. Could it be that the love of Christ, mysterious and imperceptible as the coming of the dawn, was already beginning to warm and lighten the deep darkness of his broken heart? He hardly knew; but he spread his cloak round his slave and drew him to his side. Then, thankful that the streets were still completely deserted, they hurried home to sleep.

8

PHILEMON SLEPT TILL ELEVEN AND THEN woke with a start. He must not be late. They would be gathering in the school room, and he must not miss a word. He felt like a child standing on the edge of a vast shoreless ocean of Life and Love and Truth. Paul had spoken of the love of Christ that passeth knowledge, but today he would at least begin to know a little, and they would all go on together, he and his son and his slaves. The Son of God had loved them too and given Himself for them, and they must hear and understand.

Archippus, recovered after a good night's sleep, was waiting impatiently in the atrium, and he, too, took one look at his father and knew. A terrible feeling of loneliness swept over him, for his father had gone ahead where he could not follow, and the holiday to which he had so looked forward was ruined. Deep in his heart, unacknowledged even to himself, was horror and disgust at what he had sensed in the temple, and yet he had heard enough of Christianity to know that it cut right across worldly ease and prosperity, popularity and the usual methods employed in money-making and getting on in business. Besides, it involved confessing and forsaking sin, and Archippus had every reason to avoid that. He stood staring miserably, until Philemon bade him get ready, and all four started up the hill. But it was not easy going. The crowds flocking in the direction of the theatre were in a fanatical mood, muttering, lowering and cat-calling, and had not Paul been accompanied by two stalwart muscular Macedonians, he would hardly have reached the school in safety. As it was, his group of intimate friends was smaller than usual; for Fortunatos, Achaicus and Stephanas, bearing the precious letter to the church of Corinth, were already down at the harbour enquiring about a ship bound for Greece.

But at last they were there, and the gallant little teacher stood up on the dais, breathless, mud bespattered, a swelling bruise on his forehead and the light of God in his eyes. Perhaps he knew that the time was short, for he spoke with an urgency that could not be mistaken. Was there any man present whose loyalties were divided, who had any hope or trust for this world or the next in any but Christ, Christ by Whom all things were created and in Whom all things consist, Christ in Whom are hid all the treasures of wisdom and knowledge? If so, let him acknowledge it and turn away from it forever, lest he be found a castaway.

There was a sudden stir in the audience, and a white-faced man pushed to the front and flung down a scroll at the Apostle's feet. "I have lived by my magic arts," he whispered, "but now let me cling to the power of Christ."

Only a whisper, but it was picked up and carried along the packed ranks of people. A woman burst into tears and made her way forward and flung down a silver charm.

"Burn this," said Paul vehemently. "What fellowship has light with darkness, what has Christ to do with idols, or the power of the Spirit with the power of Satan? Oh, my children in Christ, if any more of you are harbouring idolatry..."

His voice was drowned, for the whole room was astir. Quietly, and without undue confusion, men, women and children were pressing forward, while others made way. Many were weeping bitterly as they flung down idols, souvenirs of the goddesses, charms and scrolls. Philemon came forward without hesitation, but he was not weeping. His face was aglow with an unearthly radiance. For the first he was letting go of all else, to take hold of Christ with both hands. He drew the two Ephesian letters and the silver images from his wallet and laid them on the growing pile.

"Bring a brazier and fire," commanded Paul, and Gaius and Aristarchus, the Macedonians, went to a nearby house and brought what was needed. One by one the scrolls and books and letters were added to the flames, and silver charms and idols were melted down for the work of God. There was no more preaching that day. Many of the congregation had gone home and returned with cherished symbols of heathenism, and all through the afternoon the fire burned, and Gaius and Aristarchus fed the flames and carried away the ashes. It was not the first time this had happened, and they were used to the work. Not long before, they had publicly destroyed magic books and charms to the value of fifty thousand pieces of silver; but more and more were believing and being drawn to trust in Christ, and Christ alone.

But the smoke was straying out through the windows, and when at last the company left the hall, they were met by ominous muttering and black looks. Mercifully, most people were either sleeping through the hot hour or collecting round the theatre, but even so the boys were glad to reach home in safety, gladder still to set out with the crowd, after a meal, to watch the wrestling bouts, although Philemon refused to accompany them.

"I shall return to Paul," he said. "The time may be short. He cannot survive the Artemisia in safety."

Philemon was right. The time was very short. The news was sweeping round the frenzied city: "They have burned the scrolls and melted the idols." And by the third day it was impossible to reach the precincts of the school. Philemon sat for hours with Paul in the weaving shed, and the boys roamed the streets and saw plays and contests to their heart's content; but they knew the muttering thunder clouds must soon break, and Archippus feared desperately for his father.

"Father," he said, late on the evening of the third day, when Philemon, under cover of darkness, had just returned from Aquila and Priscilla's house, "shall we not go back to Colosse? You seem to have lost interest in the guilds, and my mother will be lonely."

"We shall soon go, my son," answered his father. "It cannot be long now. The storm must break very soon, and I want to be with Paul when it comes."

"Well, I don't," answered Archippus, beginning to panic. "Why throw away your life, father? Think of mother and little Pascasia and me."

"I do not think I shall lose my life," said Philemon quietly. "Have I not just begun to serve Christ? Has He not called me to carry the Gospel to Colosse? But to suffer for him would be great gain. If we suffer, we shall reign with Him. Oh, my son, if you knew..."

"I know, I know, but I don't want to know!" burst out

Archippus. "Father, this way of life is not for me. Please do not speak to me any more about it. Come, Onesimus, we will go up to the theatre."

They started off, idly enough. In spite of what his father had done, Archippus still intended to take home some souvenirs, especially for little Mistress Eirene whom he was planning to visit as soon as possible. They wandered along the street of the silversmiths in the direction of the temple; but after they had gone a little way they found that the crowd were so dense that they could hardly force their way through.

"What is happening?" asked Archippus. "There must be some sort of public meeting. Look, there is Demetrius, the silversmith, standing on a corn bushel in front of his shop, addressing a crowd. Can you hear what he is saying, Onesimus? He seems greatly excited about something."

Onesimus pressed forward, straining his ears to hear what the gesticulating man was holding forth about. But suddenly the words were drowned by a tremendous shout from the throng. The whole street seemed to sway, and the words rose in a deafening roar, "Great ... great ... great is Diana of the Ephesians. Down with Paul! The temple of the great goddess Diana is in danger of being destroyed. They have burned the scrolls and thrown her images into the fire. Great ... great ... great is Diana of the Ephesians."

The whole affair had got out of control. It was no longer an indignation meeting of the silversmiths, but a mob gone mad. Like a threatening sea wave they all began to move in one direction, jostling, screaming, eyes dilated, teeth snarling, carrying all before them. Both boys were caught up, helpless in the surging tide of humanity, and they found themselves borne up the hill towards the theatre, half deafened by the monotonous cry, "Great is Diana ... great is Diana ... great is Diana of the Ephesians."

Onesimus got separated from his young master, but he could still see him between the shoulders of the crowd, for he was a tall boy. Archippus looked thoroughly scared, and as if to protect himself from suspicion, he was screaming his loudest, "Great is Diana ...," and suddenly Onesimus found himself despising Archippus as a coward. Although no word had passed between them, each boy knew how the other had felt about the visit to the temple, each knew what the other had seen, and only two days before Archippus had watched his father fling down the scrolls and images. Yet here he was, screaming himself hoarse for Diana. Onesimus looked away in disgust.

Then suddenly he sensed an opportunity, and the triumph of the moment was so sweet that he almost forgot the yelling surging crowd round him. His young master was, at that moment, completely in his power, and his revenge was within easy reach. At first he recoiled from the idea, but it forced itself back on him. Every insult and slight and humiliation he had endured, every undeserved punishment, all the years of forced, unwilling obedience, and above all, the memory of himself being beaten with rods for the crime Archippus had committed, rose up before him in a deadly pageant. Half stupid with heat, noise and confusion, he turned to the nearest rioter and whispered as he pointed, "His father burnt the Ephesian letters two days ago."

The moment he had said the words he would have given his life to recall them, but it was too late. His whisper was like a spark dropped on dry tinder, and within seconds all those nearest to Archippus had turned on him, hissing, shrieking, shaking their fists. "His father burnt the letters! Son of a blasphemer! Down with these Christ followers! Great is Diana!"

Someone had struck him in the face, and another had got hold of his hair. Onesimus just caught a glimpse of his ashen face, his mouth open wide in vain protest. "Great is Diana!" he shrieked, and then the mob closed in on him and he was down, trampled, dying under their feet.

"Christ save me! Christ save me!" he screamed. It was his last desperate appeal in the darkness as he fell, and two men who had been caught up against their will by the mob heard the cry. Gaius the Macedonian, strong as an ox, was scattering men right and left, flailing his arms like a windmill in his efforts to reach the spot. A blow here and a well-aimed kick there, and he had cleared a space and dragged the unconscious lad from beneath the feet of the crowd.

The original agitators had been swept ahead, Onesimus among them, and in the noise and confusion no one on the spot knew why the boy had been knocked down. A hush fell over those nearest as the limp, bleeding figure was passed back to Aristarchus, who was just behind, and who, laying the boy on his stalwart shoulders, struggled to gain a side street. This being impossible, he had to be content with lifting the quiet form over the heads of the mob, where it was passed from one to another until it reached the outskirts.

Onesimus had been carried on up the hill, and his last

sight of Archippus had been his face when the crowd closed in upon him and he fell. "Archippus is dead," he was saying to himself, and everything else was an evil dream, far away and unimportant. Somehow he was pushed, unresisting, into the theatre and was vaguely surprised when Paul's two sturdy friends, Gaius and Aristarchus, were dragged on to the platform, bruised, buffetted and in danger of being lynched. They had drawn too much attention to themselves in their efforts to save the boy and had been recognised and mobbed.

It might have been an hour, or a day, or two days that Onesimus crouched amidst the shrieking, sweating throng and watched that fool Alexander waving his ineffectual hand for silence and mouthing words that the man next to him could not have heard. Then, a long, long time after, there was a silence like the silence of death, and the town clerk stood up and said something. Onesimus neither knew nor cared what it was, although he was told later that it was a brilliant speech. Day, night, tumult or silence, all was the same to him; for only one thing mattered any more forever: Archippus was dead, and he had killed him.

9

IT HAD NEVER ENTERED HIS HEAD THAT Archippus could die. A couple of black eyes, and a few teeth knocked out was about all he had imagined, and he would have enjoyed that. A country boy straight from the mountains, he had no knowledge of mob madness, but it was no good regretting now. Archippus was dead, trampled under the feet of the crowd, and the night had fallen and the shouting had ceased. He was standing under the stars, outside the theatre which he had left because everyone else had left. The town clerk had ordered all festivities to stop and the streets to be cleared for fear of further riots; so he was quite alone, and there was nowhere to stay and nowhere to go.

He could not go back to his master, and anyhow, where was he? Mourning beside the body of his son, or searching the streets for him? Onesimus looked all round him, as though searching for some refuge - to the mountains on his left with the fierce stars burning above them, to the moonlit marshes on his right, to the sleeping white city below him and the silver sea beyond. If he could run to the harbour and slip over the side beneath the waves perhaps he could find rest and oblivion. But into whose arms would he be committing himself? Neither Diana or Christ, nor any of the other deities had stretched out a hand to save Archippus. Perhaps there was no one, nothing, and to fall into darkness and nothingness alone with his sin was a terrible thought. It was better even to face life than to face death or some angry unknown god.

Nothing. No one. Unconsciously his feet had been carrying him past the theatre and down the hill towards Philemon's house. Now he was standing at the end of their street, and he suddenly longed for his master who had been, in spite of it all, a good master. Then it occurred to him that his master need never know. He could still go back and pretend to be horrified at the news. No one need ever know. Everything could go on as before, except for the torment of his own guilty conscience. He quickened his steps and reached the house, and knocked. But the door was locked and the house was empty.

Nothing. No one. He must find some kind human being, someone he could touch and see and hear. He longed for his mother, but his mother was far, far away at the foot of the gorges where the flocks grazed. It seemed like another world. Then he remembered the weaver's wife with her smile and her gentle hands. He would go there and ask if there was any news of his master.

He ran all the way, down the harbour street and up the side alley, and there was a glimmer of light shining from the weaving shed. It, too, was locked, and at first no one answered his timid knock, although he could hear someone moving about inside. He knocked again, and after a little while a frightened voice said, "Who is there?"

"I, the slave who supped with you the other night. Oh, Mistress Priscilla, let me in!"

The door was opened cautiously. He slipped inside and Priscilla slammed it shut. She was very pale, and she looked as if she had been weeping, but when she saw the grey strained face of the boy and the fear in his eyes, she forgot her own troubles.

"Why, child, what is the matter?" she asked. "Did you get caught in the riots, too?"

He stared at her in silence. His heart was breaking and he longed to tell her all about it and cry his heart out against her, but he must never, never tell anyone. He suddenly realised that all his life he would have to carry this secret alone, a great barrier between him and every other human being; so he simply answered, "Yes, I was in the riots. I am looking for my master. Have you seen him?"

Priscilla shook her head and drew Onesimus into the inner room where she was busy packing the provisions. She was glad to have someone to talk to, and she could see that the boy needed to rest. She laid him on a couch and brought him bread and wine, chatting away all the time.

"I have not seen your master. I expect he is with the other disciples up at the school of Tyrannus, and I only hope they will have the sense to stop talking before it is too late. Paul would go and say farewell to them all. Crazy, I call it, but you cannot stop him. It was all we could do to prevent him from going to the theatre and putting himself right into their hands! He, our father in Christ! Gaius and Aristarchus were caught and barely escaped with their lives. They are covered with bruises from head to foot, but they are strong as bulls and it won't hurt them. But they must leave the town with Paul and be out and away on the coast road for Macedonia before dawn. They could never get past the temple alive after daylight. They will look in here to collect food for the journey soon after midnight, they said. Stay here if you like, child and rest. You look as though you need it."

He was grateful to obey. If his master was really up at the school there was no point following him, and if he was not, Onesimus had no idea where else to look for him. Besides he felt too tired ever to move again. The wine had been strong and sweet, and merciful sleep was stealing over him. Just for a little while he could forget. He closed his eyes, and she covered him with a blanket, prayed that the Lord would give him light, and went back to her baking.

He woke up suddenly, some hours later. It was still dark, although the first cock was crowing and the room was full of whispering men who seemed in a hurry; but his master was not amongst them

Peering over his blanket, Onesimus watched their tense faces in the lamp light as they made their last hasty preparations for flight. Gaius was there, with his head in bandages, and Aristarchus' face was twice its normal size; but they seemed strong and impatient to be on their way. Staves in hand, faces hidden in rough hoods, they were all setting out together to escort Paul through the dangerous temple suburbs and on to the coast road.

"Is Philemon the Colossian not with you?" asked Priscilla. "His slave came searching for him. He is over there, asleep."

"He did not come," said Paul, his voice very sad. "How deeply I longed to say farewell, for he is my dearly beloved son in the faith. What can have happened, I wonder, to keep him from us tonight?"

Of all the company, Paul alone seemed in no hurry. He

crossed over to where Onesimus lay and stood looking down on him, his scarred face very tender.

"Tell him I sought for him and longed for him," he said. "Tell him I commend him to God and to the grace of our Lord Jesus Christ. Tell him I pray continually that he may be strengthened with might by God's spirit in the inner man. Bid him to carry the Gospel of Christ to his valley where my feet have never trod. And you, my son..."

He was soaring away in spirit, forgetful of time or place, all his thoughts with his new-born child in the faith, who had not come. The waiting company fidgeted nervously, for the darkness was thinning and Gaius and Aristarchus were particularly conspicuous. Priscilla laid her hand on his arm.

"Our father in Christ," she said firmly, "the cocks are crowing all over the town."

He came back to them at once, and smiled at this staunch faithful woman who for over two years had stood by him through thick and thin and served him and fed him and cared for him as he battled with his persecutors, travailed over his converts and worked day and night to train the evangelists who were to carry the news all over western Asia. She had baked all night and loaded them now with at least three days' provisions. He turned to bless little Levi where he lay asleep; but he somehow felt himself being propelled through the door by Mistress Priscilla. Already the grey light was stealing down the street and there was not a moment to lose. He turned to bless her for the last time, but she had gone inside and shut the door, fearful of further delay. Sitting at the loom where Paul had worked for his living, although they would so gladly have supported him, Priscilla buried her face in her hands and wept.

"O Father," she prayed, "take them unharmed on their journey; keep Thy Church in this town, and bring my dear Aquila safely home."

Onesimus watched her for a time and then went over to her. "I must go and find my master," he said. "It will be light now, and I think he will have come home."

She wiped away her tears and let him out into the street, telling him not to forget the Apostle's parting message to his master. He turned the corner and glanced seaward, but there was no glory of sunrise today! The morning was stealing in wrapped in a grey mist, and he suddenly remembered how his master had wrapped his cloak around him and drawn him to his side on that last chilly dawn. He began to run up the harbour street, longing and yet dreading to get back to him, expecting to hear the sound of wailing and mourning coming from the windows. But the door was still locked and the house was empty.

Where was Philemon? Was he dead too? And where was Hermes? Were they all dead? In a sudden panic he crashed at the neighbour's door with such force that the whole family came running to the door, rubbing the sleep from their eyes and gaping.

"My master!" cried Onesimus before they had a chance to tell him what they thought of him. "Do you know where he is? I can't find him!"

"Well, no need to break our door down, if you can't!" growled the owner of the house. "Your master will keep. However, as a matter of fact I do know where he is, and he left a message for you. His son was injured in the riots and taken to hospital up above the Agora, and he is up there with him. He said you were to go and wait on him."

Onesimus' relief was so great that he nearly fainted. A hospital was for the living, not for the dead. Could it be...? He dared not even think of it lest he be disappointed; yet hope seemed to wing his young feet as he sped across the market place and up the hill to the south of the city. And even as he ran the sun rose over the crest to meet him, bathing the marble pillars, temples and city buildings in a rosy light.

Life! Life! The relief was so great that he forgot the possibility of pain or weakness or of deformity worse than death. He found the hospital without any difficulty and almost pushed aside the porter who wanted to know his business. His business was with his master, and a moment later he bounded into the quiet hall where several who had been crushed or injured in the riots lay on couches. A woman sat weeping beside a tiny child, and an old man lay very quiet, as though asleep. Onesimus checked himself, and his joy drained away as he caught sight of Philemon and Hermes sitting motionless beside a still figure on a couch in the corner.

So very, very still. His head was tied up in blood-stained bandages, and his face, apart from the deep blue bruises, was white as death. They all seemed to be sitting there waiting for death, yet outside the sun had risen and the darkness had passed. Onesimus crouched at this master's feet and looked up yearningly into his face. Philemon leaned forward.

"Go to the weaver's house," he said, "and entreat the Apostle to come. Tell him my son is grievously wounded."

91

"But the Apostle has gone," interrupted Onesimus. "He went before daybreak on the road to Macedonia. I saw him go."

Philemon sprang up. "Gone!" he repeated. "And I never saw him or bade him farewell. Oh, why should this have happened? He could have healed Archippus. They say there was healing in the very garments and handkerchiefs that he touched, and even devils were cast out, and to think I missed him!"

"But the Christ he told us about is still here." Archippus opened his eyes at the sound of their voices and spoke feebly but distinctly. "He will not leave us. As I fell, I knew. I cried out, and He came to me. If I die I shall see Him again as I saw Him then. He spoke with difficulty, for he had been drugged with wine and myrrh to ease his pain, and everything seemed far away except the Presence that had come to him as he struggled under the feet of the crowd and had lifted him up. The arms of Aristarchus and the arms of Christ - perhaps they were one and the same, for was He not alive in His people and working through their dedicated members? But Archippus only understood that a long time afterwards. On that day he knew that Christ Himself had heard his cry and had stooped down and lifted him from the gates of death.

His father leaned forward and spoke to him in a low voice, and he closed his eyes and seemed to drop into unconsciousness. But he was restless and after a time he spoke again.

"Father, Onesimus, I *must* tell you. I cannot die unforgiven. *I* stole the chain from Master Plautus that day in Colosse, and I let Onesimus be beaten with rods for my sin."

There was a long moment of shocked silence. Then Philemon spoke slowly but firmly: "As Christ died and suffered for your sin, it is forgiven, my son. He bore it; He made peace by the blood of His Cross."

"Yes," whispered Archippus, "I know. But I want you to forgive me, too."

"I do forgive you, my son," said his father. But Onesimus, remembering the rods, was silent.

10

THE WOUNDS ON ARCHIPPUS' HEAD SOON healed up, for he was young and strong, but his leg had been twisted and trampled on and was badly broken. He suffered agonies at the hands of the surgeons and bone setters, and it was some weeks before he could move from his bed, except to be carried to the house, and then it was clear to all that he would never walk again without limping, for one of his legs was shortened and deformed.

Hermes was sent to Colosse to carry the news to Apphia, and Onesimus waited on his young master day and night. Archippus did not change in a day. His suffering and helplessness and the increasing heat often made him exceedingly irritable and bad-tempered, yet there was a difference. He seemed to recognise that Onesimus was a person with a soul of his own and a right of his own to live, instead of being Archippus' property, born with no other purpose but to serve him. Onesimus was often amazed and embarrassed at his young master's humility and gentleness and even gratitude, and at his penitence when his suffering made him difficult and impatient. He hardly knew how to deal with this relationship and was thankful to get away and run along the hillside to the southern beaches, and there fling himself into the sparkling Aegean. He would swim far, far out, enjoying the cool water and his own fine strength, forgetting the troubling thoughts that so often assailed him.

"You are young and strong," the lazy blue water seemed to tell him, "and this life is fair, and death and judgment are far away. Enjoy what you have here and now, for the narrow way that leads to Eternal Life is not for you. Archippus paid the price, but it is a price you could never pay. So eat and drink and be merry, and love the sun and the sea, and worship the beauty of the earth."

And for Archippus and Philemon the hours were not dull; for the little church at Ephesus rallied round them. Priscilla became the boy's faithful nurse, cooking appetising dishes and dressing his wounds, and from morning till night there were small groups of Christians gathered at his bedside. Through the long, hot summer hours they told him the story of Christ, of the old Jewish prophecies, of His lowly birth, His spotless life, His atoning death and His glorious resurrection, of the coming of the Holy Spirit at Pentecost, and of the Gospel they had been chosen to proclaim. Philemon had lost all interest in the guilds now. His farm was prospering in any case, and his aim in life was to carry the Gospel to his valley and to help build up the Church of Christ in Colosse, in Laodicea and in Hieropolis, and perhaps even to join Epaphras on his travels northwards to Sardis, to Pergamos and the other great cities of Asia. His heart was aglow with the spring-time of his early love, and there was so much to learn if he was to lead others. Often they would sit talking far into the night, until the sky and the stars seemed no barrier to the heavenly places where they roamed in spirit.

Visitors from other districts and lands often dropped in, for most ships stopped at Ephesus where three great roads converged, and many were the stories told round Archippus' couch.

Unless the story was thrilling enough to keep him awake, Onesimus, however, usually fell asleep during these discourses, for he had no interest in the spread of the Gospel. Besides his mind was beginning to be full of other schemes for his own future. Hermes had not returned, for he was directing the hay-making at the farm, and Philemon, with his older slave away and his son crippled, was giving Onesimus more and more responsibility. He went daily to the market on small errands, and he felt that Philemon, with his head in the clouds dreaming of Christ's glory, was not likely to check carefully on the price of a melon or a joint of meat. The coins he was hiding away were very small indeed, but they were mounting up and he was still young. One day his time would come. He must be patient, always patient, and very, very careful.

It was high summer when Archippus was at last ready to be carried home to Colosse and the travelling would be arduous because of the heat. They hired a flat cart with an awning, drawn by oxen, and the crippled boy lay on a bed. He looked white and wasted and was longing for his mother and the higher cooler air of the Colossian plateau, but they were all sorry to leave their friends in Ephesus. Many accompanied them on their way when they set off in the dark over the wall of Mount Prion and turned to take a long look at the beautiful white sleeping city, before dropping down into a sandy valley where the warm air was scented with pines and junipers. At length the path led up to the fertile river pastures where the grey light was beginning to steal down, and on and on they went, loth to part: Aquila, with little Levi riding joyfully on the oxen, Onesiphorus, Epaenetus and all the others whose brothers they had become and whom they had learned to love with that deep, new love of the Spirit within them.

Then the sun appeared over the mountains that walled in the valley ahead, lifting the heads of the sunflowers and poppies and kissing the young green corn into gold. They stopped under a group of poplar trees that screened them from the road and sang the hymn that Paul had taught them, with tears of mingled joy and fear streaming down their faces:

"If we died with Him,
We shall also live with Him:
If we suffer,
We shall also reign with Him:
If we deny Him,
He will also deny us."

Death and suffering. They were round them on all sides like thunder clouds about to break, but in the flush of his young, untried courage, Philemon felt no fear of either. He was going home to his wife and to his great new adventure, to win the valley for Christ. They parted with prayers and blessing and went on their way rejoicing.

But it was a difficult journey. The air under the awning was stifling in the day time, and Archippus, tormented by flies and heat and the jolting of the wagon, became as irritable and imperious as he had ever been in his life; and Onesimus, forced to wait on him, did so with a sullen stony resentment that was worse than outright cruelty.

And yet Onesimus was not unhappy. If Archippus was so unpleasant and unjust, then he had little sympathy with his sufferings, and he was glad to be going home. Lately he had tired of the noisy city streets and the buzz of the harbour, and he longed for the silence of the mountains and for the pools and streams and rocks of the canyons. The dancing poppies, the green corn sighing and bowing in the wind, the hundreds of small, brave flowers along the wayside, the glorious dawns and sunsets and the wide spaces of stars over the mountain crests captivated him with their beauty. He loved travelling. The world was very wide, and men even spoke of lands beyond the Roman Empire. When he was free he would travel to the utmost bounds and beyond.

They reached their own familiar valley late on the fourth day. The air was beginning to cool, and they hoped to arrive home before dark. These long June evenings were the best time to travel and Archippus had just waked from sleep and was lying quietly on his side, watching the landscape bathed in the golden light of the late afternoon. His father had walked ahead, and Onesimus lay prone, his chin cupped in his hands. They were about to pass under the fortifications of Laodicea and he was gazing up at them, dreaming. In which house did she live and what was she doing just now? Had she grown and changed, or was she still the same simple, kindly, merry little maiden? He had often thought of her at Ephesus. In fact she was always there in the back of his mind, but now he suddenly began to realize all she had meant to him and made him. It was because of her innocence and purity that he had known instantly that the temple worship of Artemis was vile and ugly; it was because of her young, slender body, held so proudly, that he had known that life and youth were glorious as he swam in the sea; it was her innate beauty that had opened his eyes to all beauty and made the flowers along the way and the colours of the sky things of joy and worship. He longed for her now with a new distinct longing, and a resolve was suddenly born in him to see her again as soon as might be.

"I'm sorry, Onesimus, I'm sorry," Archippus' voice, humble and pleading, broke in upon his thoughts. He did not wish to think about Archippus and his problems just then, but he supposed he had better listen, so he called back over his shoulder assuring him that all was well.

"But it's not all well," said Archippus. He was tired out with the journey and disappointment at his own bad behaviour, weary with trying to be brave. "Oh, Onesimus, I wish you were a Christian, and then you would understand and pray for me instead of hating me when I'm hard and unkind. Christ taught us to suffer patiently, but I fail all the time."

Onesimus rolled over and gaped at him. He could not begin to understand this new Archippus. "I don't hate you," he said awkwardly. "I'm sorry for you. Probably we feel the same sometimes. You are held by your injury and I am held by my slavery. But one day maybe your Christ or your Paul will heal you. They say he did many miracles. And one day, maybe, I shall buy my freedom, so there is hope for us both."

"Do you hate being a slave so much then?" asked Archippus softly. He had never thought about it before. "I think it would not matter so much if you were a Christian. Aquila used to say that in Christ there was neither bond nor free. He taught us to bear Christ's yoke with meekness and to be content with our lot, as Paul is content with prison and stripes and hunger and thirst and danger. But oh, Onesimus may God forgive me and Christ have mercy upon me, I am not content with my lot."

"Neither am I," said Onesimus. He had no intention of bearing his yoke with meekness or of being content with his lot. He fingered the little lump on the inside of the girdle where he had hoarded his coins and smiled to himself. One day he would change his lot.

11

ONESIMUS' RESOLVE WAS MADE MORE difficult by the fact that Philemon's friendship with Polemon came to an abrupt end.

A few days after the party from Ephesus had arrived Polemon came over to talk business and enquire about the guilds. Philemon explained that he had not been able to join the guilds. How could he, as a Christian, take part in their feasts and eat the food offered to idols and bind himself to the brotherhood by sacrificing to gods? He talked to Polemon about Christ and this very greatly offended the rich merchant. He left the house quickly, saying he desired no hospitality from a lunatic and would enquire at the Laodicean medical school about a potion for brain fever. But he continued to buy Philemon's wool because it was the best in the valley.

All through the hot fruitful days Philemon attended to his harvesting, and Epaphras remained in Colosse. Onesimus ran between the threshing floor, the winepress, the olive yards and Archippus. But although Archippus longed for his strong young companionship more than ever, he did not need him as before. For one thing, he had learned to walk with a crutch and was becoming quite independent, and for another, his mother and little Pascasia competed with each other to wait on him hand and foot. Also, he had started to study the Jewish scriptures and was already beginning to take his place as a preacher.

For night after night when the work of the day was finished and the dusk had fallen, the people began to arrive, stealing up from the town and in from the pastures; and a strangely assorted crowd would gather in the atrium: shepherds and reapers smelling of the flocks and the fields, tired slaves, women and little children, dignified merchants and a group of exiled Jews. Among these were two or three keen-eyed Rabbis with their Pentateuchs and scrolls of history tucked under their arms. These had been but old stories of dead men and but revered words from the past, until they had suddenly discovered Christ blazing out from every parchment. Now, night after night, they pored over them, tracing the signs of His coming, reading new, living interpretations into words that had hitherto been dead. The slaves and the labourers and the mothers would soon slip out, overcome by sleep and much learning, but Philemon, Epaphras and the Rabbis would sometimes continue until the stars paled.

There was little opposition at that time. Everyone was too busy getting in the harvests. The Rabbis were excommunicated from their synagogues for teaching heresy and consorting with unclean Gentiles; but they felt drawn to unclean Gentiles and did not greatly care. Philemon was highly respected in the town and was left to do as he pleased. But from other cities, where Epaphras had preached the Gospel and founded small churches, there came rumours of persecution and fear of death.

"The olives are in," said Epaphras to Philemon, as they

sat one noonday enjoying the golden autumn sunlight, " the harvests are stored. I should like you to come with me on my trip north and encourage and exhort our suffering brethren."

"And who will care for the church here," asked Philemon. Epaphras' gaze rested thoughtfully on Archippus who was sitting a little way apart struggling with his longing to go too. "I think you, Archippus, could start to undertake that ministry, with the help of the Rabbis," he said. "You are young, but the Lord is giving you much light."

"Me!" Archippus looked up, flushed with pleasures at the older man's words. "But Master Epaphras, I know so little yet!"

"The Holy Spirit shall teach you all things, and bring to your remembrance what you have learned," quoted Epaphras. "These were the very words of Jesus. And you have the Scriptures. Now, take heed to your ministry."

He smiled at the amazed boy and turned back to Philemon, and Onesimus, clearing away the meal, pricked up his ears.

"We will pass by Laodicea," he said "for the Christians meeting in the house of Nymphas are mostly rich, prosperous and respected and seem to need no help. In Hieropolis they are firmly grounded in the faith. In Philadelphia they stand fast. But in Sardis they are in danger of being defiled. The streets of that city flow with gold, and the vice and loose-living and shame that prevail are unbelievable. I pray God they will keep their garments white. In Thyatira they have been excluded from the trade guilds and are in deep poverty. But in Pergamos and Smyrna, where Caesar is worshipped and the sacrifice to Nero is compulsory, they are in daily danger of losing their lives. Yes, I must be off. I should like to start tomorrow at daybreak."

So next day the two men started off together down the valley, staves in hand, their bundles on their backs, without slaves or attendants; and Apphia and Archippus took over the direction of the household. Onesimus in the meantime began to scheme and plan for a day's escape at whatever cost, when suddenly fate played into his hands.

Pascasia had been playing out in the field, picking berries in the hedges, and had rubbed her eyes with some poisonous juice. She came in crying, her eyes sore and inflamed, and by evening she could hardly see. Apphia was deeply anxious.

"Hermes must go over to Laodicea early tomorrow morning," she said " and buy some of the Laodicean eye-salve. Go and tell him to start before day-break, Onesimus, and give him the money."

Onesimus stopped outside the house to consider. He had wild thoughts of attacking Hermes, tripping him up, or knocking him senseless; but after a moment or two he decided that persuasion was better than force. He darted home and took the smallest of his precious coins from its hiding place and sought out Hermes who was busy cleaning the stables.

"Hermes," he began, holding out the coin, "look what I will give you to be ill tomorrow."

Hermes stared at him and his rather stupid mouth fell open. Then he stared at the coin.

"Where did you get that from?" he asked suspiciously.

"Never you mind! I earned it at Ephesus. It will buy you a basin of honey to make you fatter, Hermes. But you've got to be too ill to go to Laodicea tomorrow. I want to go instead."

Hermes stared doubtfully at the impudent young cockerel hopping about impatient at the older man's stupidity. Hermes was fat and lazy and hated being sent to Laodicea. Besides, he had not possessed a coin for years. But he was not sure that he knew how to be ill, for he had never been ill in his life.

"Scream, Hermes," urged Onesimus. "Vomit! Say you've overeaten and groan as loud as you can. They'll all believe that. By the time they discover the truth, I shall be half way down the hill."

"And I shall be beaten," muttered Hermes. But the sight of the coin was so attractive and the prospect of a twenty mile walk so unattractive, that he agreed to the plan without much more ado. Besides, he suddenly remembered that Philemon was away and Apphia disliked beatings.

Onesimus took no chances. He started off in the dark long before sunrise, while the household was still asleep, merely leaving a message that as Hermes had been very ill in the night, he, Onesimus, had gone instead.

He could hardly believe his good fortune as he dipped down over the edge of the first plain and the farm disappeared from view. He was safe and away, and no one could stop him now. He leapt and sang like a young mad thing, for was he not free for a whole day, and was he not going to see the child of the canyons? In his elation he never even considered the possibility of failure or the extreme unlikelihood of a slaves's managing to speak with a high-born carefully guarded little lady like Eirene. Nothing could fail today.

The sun rose as he crossed the lower plateau, but the season of burning heat was over, and its rays warmed and cheered him. All around him were golds and silvers; deep gold poplars and walnut trees and pale gold empty corn fields with their stubble and baked earth, silver of stripped olive trees and, silver in the sunlight, the river below him. The miles seemed to be rolling away, and it was still fresh morning when he reached the gates of Laodicea and passed inside its fortifications. It seemed to him an enormous, magnificent city, almost an equal with Ephesus.

And certainly Laodicea was a fine city. Destroyed by an earthquake forty years before, it had been rebuilt in modern style with wide streets, three fine new theatres and a gymnasium. It was the seat of all banking arrangements for Asia and notoriously wealthy, for it was also the centre for the wool industry, and the clothes and fabrics woven in the Laodicean factories were exported all over the Empire. Onesimus went straight to the Apothecary who lived in the shadow of the great medical school and bought a box of the tephra-Phrygia, the world famous eye powder of Laodicea. Then, his errand accomplished, he started off to find Eirene's home.

This was not difficult. The weavers in the cloth factories all knew Polemon, and one pointed out his great marble mansion up on the hill by the Hieropolis gate. Only when he reached the outer portals and saw the beautiful house enclosed in an acre of garden, did he begin to realize how foolish he had been to imagine he could ever reach her.

But he could not, he would not, give up. If he could just get a little nearer to the house! A bold idea struck him, and he marched up to the door with his head held high. "Master Philemon of Colosse sends greetings to Master Polemon of Laodicea," he announced firmly to the slave at the portal, "and begs to inform him that the next bale of wool will soon be dispatched. He would also have news of his health and the health of his daughter, the Mistress Eirene."

"Tell him," said the slave, "that Master Polemon has ridden to Thyatira to buy purple dye, but he will be back in two days' time. He and his daughter both prosper and are in good health."

Well, there was nothing to do now but to turn round and go away; but if Polemon was not at home, he could take his time. He wandered slowly toward the gate, looking back over his shoulder at the great house; and then, suddenly, as he glanced toward the garden, he saw her, crouching on the ground under a mulberry tree, gathering mulberries into a basket.

As before, he saw her a full minute before she saw him, and he noticed that she had changed very little. She was still slender, although probably taller, and her dark hair still fell loose about her face and shoulders. But there was a grave lonely air about her, and when she stood up to reach the great twisted bough, she looked strangely small and fragile. All his shyness left him. He threw caution to the winds and sped over the grass toward her.

She looked up quickly, and all her gravity disappeared. She knew him instantly, and her face dimpled into a delightful smile.

"Have you not forgotten me, Mistress Eirene?" he asked her.

How could she ever forget him? Had he not been the hero of the one and only adventure she had ever had in her dull, lonely little life? Since the death of her mother the days had all been exactly alike: the correct programme of meals, lessons, embroidery and a well protected walk or an hour's play in the garden. But at night when she lay in bed and had bidden her correct nurse a correct goodnight and had said what she was expected to say to her father, her thoughts would fly back to the canyon at Colossse, and, half-asleep and half-awake, she would go climbing on with the boy to where flowers of unimaginable beauty bent their heads to bright streams. Sometimes the path was too steep for her or the boulders too high, and then the boy would give her his hand and help her, and it was always more beautiful further on. They never got to the top, not even in her dreams; but one day, together, they would look over the other side. So she studied, and did as she was told, and stayed where she should and everyone called her a good obedient little maid. But her spirit lived in another country, where the streams were cold and the rocks were high and the snows not far away; and no one had ever followed her there, except the boy who was always with her.

And here he was again, and she was not dreaming. He was taller and thinner, his face a little more angular but not really changed. He was looking at her in just the same way with the same merry light of adventure in his eyes. To her it did not matter at all that he was a slave; but she knew that other people did not share her opinions and she looked anxiously towards the house.

"Come to the herb garden," she said quickly, taking his hand, just as she had taken it in the canyon. "Down there, behind these cypress trees no one can see us, and if my governess comes you can get behind the bushes."

They sat down together among the sweet smelling herbs and shrubs, where the sun was hot and golden and the bees hummed in and out of the bushes, and smiled delightedly at each other. "Do you remember that deep pool where you found me?" she asked, as though it had happened yesterday. "And do you remember how cross my nurse was? My father sent her away because she let me get lost, and I was glad, because she was never kind to me. Now I have a governess, and that is much better. She does not care much what I do, as long as I finish my lessons and stay in the garden."

"I had hoped you would come over to Colosse again," said Onesimus, "and we might have escaped up the canyon. Do you remember how that slave of yours hit me? It was well worth it!"

"We shall not come again," said Eirene, suddenly grown grave and thoughtful. "My father would not take me the last time he went there, because I had run away that day, and he came back very angry indeed. He said your master had become a Christian, and he thought he must have lost his senses. I heard him telling Master Molassos, his chief weaver, about it. Onesimus, have you become a Christian? Are you all Christians?"

"Not I," said Onesimus, "I want to have nothing to do with it. It seems a weak sort of religion to me - forgiving your enemies and being content with your lot. I want to fight and revenge wrong, and I want to save up and be a free man when I am older."

His eyes were flashing, and she looked at him, puzzled. Then she said, hesitantly, "But it makes people so kind. My father does not know, but we have an old shepherd who is a Christian. He worships with the people who collect in Master Nymphas' house. He and his wife live in a cottage not far from the Syrian gate where the pastures slope down to the river, and he tends my father's flock. Sometimes on my walks with Claudia, my slave, we go there. Claudia likes to look at the shops, so she leaves me in the cottage with old Euphron and Antonia. They are different from other people; they are so kind. And Antonia tells me stories about their God, Christ, how He touched a terrible leper and healed him, and took a little dead girl by the hand and she lived, and called the children to Him when everyone else was bidding them be gone."

"Eirene," said Onesimus, half teasing, "I believe you are almost a Christian yourself."

"No-o-o," said Eirene slowly. "My father would not allow me to be one. He would be angry if I even spoke of it. And yet, when I hear about this Christ, sometimes I feel that I love Him. Did Artemis or Cybele or our own god of healing, Asclepius, ever say, 'Let the little children come to me'? I think only Christ ever said that."

The bright colour had flooded her cheeks as she spoke, for she had never told anyone else these thoughts, and Onesimus knew she was showing him her inmost lonely heart. He sat very still, hardly daring to move or speak, lest he should spoil this clear moment of truth and perfect understanding. If it lasted, perhaps he, too, would show her all that was in his heart.

"Mistress Eirene! Mistress Eirene!"

She jumped up and peered round the bushes, and he crouched low. Then she turned back. "It is all right," she said. "Claudia is walking the other way. She will not come here, but I must go. Wait till I am in the house and then run behind those cypress trees to the gate; you can slip out quite easily."

Then she hesitated. How did you say goodbye to the boy who was always there in your own country at the top of the canyons? Suddenly the light of a happy memory broke across her face. "We shall meet again," she said. "Do you remember, we said that last time? And we have."

"Of course I remember," replied Onesimus. "How could I ever forget? Ye gods, wasn't your nurse cross!"

They both laughed, and she tossed back her hair and turned to run across the lawn. "Peace, peace, little Mistress Eirene," he called softly after her. "One day we shall most certainly meet again."

12

IT WAS EARLY WINTER BEFORE EPAPHRAS AND Philemon returned, full of joy and praise, and yearning to set out again as soon as possible and preach Christ where He had never been named. But although Archippus and the Rabbis had held the little church together, they were all missing their two fathers in Christ, and throughout the winter more and more turned from idols to serve the living God; and in a number of large households many of the slaves adopted their master's faith, and amongst them, Onesimus' mother.

Born into slavery, she was content to be wholly possessed by Apphia, body, soul and spirit. Life had dealt hardly with her, for her parents had belonged to a drunken brute of a master in whose household floggings and brandings were the order of the day, and, as a child, she had watched the crucifixion of a runaway slave. She had lost her three eldest children through starvation and bad treatment, and her adored husband had died as a result of a flogging. But at long last she had reached a kind mistress, and she was only too willing to follow her into this new path of peace. Not that it made much difference to her behaviour, for she had long ago learned the obedience and submission required of her; but it made a great difference to her peace of mind, for it dispelled her terrible fear of death and of an unknown future. "Come unto Me, and I will give you rest," was all that Nerissa asked of any religion, and in Christ she found it.

But with the first signs of spring, when the snow melted on the Taurus range and the passes opened and the boundaries of the world receded, a letter arrived from the elders in Ephesus, containing greetings to the churches and news of Paul. He was travelling up from Greece to Macedonia, intending to sail to Syria and keep the feast of Pentecost in Jerusalem, and he had sent a message to his dear Ephesian friends. His ship would be stopping at Miletus, about twenty miles south of Ephesus. Would they come over and meet him?

Philemon read the letter aloud to his household and looked up at the end to find Archippus kneeling in front of him, tense with anxiety.

"Father, you will take me, will you not? There is still time. Do you not remember how you hoped he would lay his hands on me and heal me? A man lame from birth was healed in the name of Jesus by Peter and John in Jerusalem, and another at the hands of Paul in Lystra. Then why not me, Father? Is the Name any less powerful for me than it was for them? Oh Father, let us start off at once, lest we be too late."

"Let us all go," said Apphia. "Pascasia is pale after the winter and the sea air will do her good, and I should dearly love to see the great apostle. You can leave Glaucus, the bailiff, in charge of the lambing and the spring sowing as you did before. He seems trustworthy and careful, and since he, too, has turned to Christ, we can count him as a brother."

Philemon hesitated. He found it hard to believe that

his dear son, who dragged himself round so painfully on a crutch, could ever again be the proud splendid creature of former years; and he struggled against his own lack of faith. Surely with God all things were possible, and if at Lystra, then why not at Miletus? He would travel to the end of the earth to seek healing for Archippus, but what if he was to be disappointed? There were many cripples in Ephesus.

"Father, Father," pleaded Archippus, "let us make ready at once. He will travel fast and we might be late."

So they made ready and set off four days later, Archippus managing to hold his excitement in check. Onesimus, much to his annoyance, was not included in the party, although his mother went to attend on Apphia and Pascasia.

"We shall soon be back," said Archippus, as he bade Onesimus goodbye. "I wish you were coming, but you are too valuable on the farm. Just think, I shall probably come back as straight as you are and go with my father when he visits the northern churches again. Why do you look like that, Onesimus? Is not the power of Christ the same as when He walked this earth, and did any go to Him in vain? Onesimus, if I am healed, will you believe in Jesus Christ?"

But the slave would make no promises. Queer things had happened in Ephesus, and Archippus might well be healed. He might even, against his will, be forced to believe with his mind, but he would never turn or commit himself to the demands of this Christ. The price was too high!

The bailiff was an old trusted slave who had recently

professed to become a Christian. He was a clever farmer and kept all in good order; but he lacked Philemon's tact and experience in dealing with slaves, and he had always been somewhat jealous of Onesimus. Now, with the boy completely in his power, he bullied and drove him from early morning till late at night, threatening him with hell fire if he ever showed signs of fatigue. Gradually a bitter feud grew up between them, carried on, on the one side, by continual scolding and oppression, and, on the other, by sullen silence, deliberate misunderstanding of orders, and probably worse. Glaucus could never prove who put salt in his wine, or lizards in his wallet, or who laid a large boulder outside his house, so that he fell headlong over it when he went home in the dark; but he had shrewd suspicions.

"I cannot abide that man," said Erastus, a keen young slave of about twenty years old, as he and Onesimus sat over their dinner one day. "Always mouthing and eating and drinking and consigning everyone else to perdition. That sort is enough to prevent anyone intelligent from turning."

"I thought you had turned yourself, and he was your brother in Christ," replied Onesimus sarcastically. "That alone would stop me becoming a Christian! Brother indeed! I'll put wormwood in his pottage tonight." He spat as far and as hard as he could.

Erastus laughed. "There is Christianity and Christianity," he said, "and we do not all accept this teaching that Christ only is the end of it all. It is too easy and simple, and it does away with all our old cultures and mysteries. By keeping our fasts and festivals and mortifying our bodies we can begin to know not only Christ and the

Holy Spirit but the Principalities and Powers, the Thrones and Dominions. There is a clever young Phrygian who has invited us to his home tonight to instruct us further, and I think you would find his teaching much more to your taste than this theory that Christ is the beginning and end of all things. It admits of some progress and scope for our intellects. All the young slaves are going. Will you come?"

"Not I!" said Onesimus shortly, "all this talk wearies me and, besides, I should fall asleep, and Glaucus would be kicking my empty bed to wake me before I was in it. He just cannot bear the thought of my getting any rest. He will suspect I am resting now, so I had better go."

But as he walked back to the house a vague idea entered his mind - only an idea at first, but he soon found it growing into a definite plan, and by the time he reached the door he had every detail arranged.

All the younger slaves were going to the Phrygian's house after dark, and he would start with them. The old slaves would sleep, and the bailiff would go to his house. Philemon's house would be guarded by large fierce dogs, every one of which was his personal friend, known since their puppyhood. It might be possible . . . . There was a stable window that opened on to the wall of the atrium, where you could catch hold of a vine branch. He had never tried, but it might be possible. There was a new moon tonight, and it would be pitch dark down there behind the stables. The old slaves slept very soundly. Not that there was much that he could steal, because all Philemon's wealth was in the Laodicean bank; but to Onesimus every tiny prize that he could store away was a step toward his goal. There was a box in Apphia's room where Pascasia kept her little trinkets, a few gold and silver bangles, some small necklaces and ear-rings. She did not often wear them now, for the Christians discouraged their womenfolk from adorning themselves, and a little girl like that would hardly remember how many she had. She would probably not even notice if one or two were missing, and later on, somewhere, they would fetch a small price.

Glaucus stood over him, growling and grumbling, as he swept out the courtyards and carried out the dirty straw from the stables. But the spring twilight fell at last, and the slaves came in from the fields and ate their supper quickly, impatient to be off.

"Where are you all going tonight?" asked Glaucus suddenly.

"Down to Alexander's house," said Erastus quickly, "Just us young ones, to praise and pray together and search the Scriptures."

"All of you?" enquired the bailiff, looking round and catching sight of Onesimus. "And you too, Onesimus? Well, I'm glad to see you taking heed and fleeing from the wrath to come. You need to think of your sins, Onesimus, for they are great. Nightly I pray for you."

"You need not waste your breath," muttered the boy rudely, but he set off with the others under Glaucus' eye. It was quite dark by now, and nobody noticed when he slipped behind an olive tree. He stood there rigidly until their voices died away, and then he was left alone with the gentle sounds of the night - the soft bleating of folded sheep, the rustling of grass and, somewhere up near the canyons, the hoot of an owl.

He crept back, his bare feet making no sound on

the cool grass, and slipped into the stable. Already the courtyard was dark and silent except for the snoring of one or two old slaves. The dogs lay with their heads on their paws, and he fondled them as he tiptoed out, so that none of them should take fright. They licked his hand and thumped their tails, for they all loved him, and he went back, curled up on some straw, rested his head against a horse's flank and waited.

It was hard work keeping awake for an hour, but at last he decided that all was safe. The old slaves would be deeply asleep by now, and the younger ones would not return till after midnight. Agile as a cat, he sprang for the window, unlatched it and squeezed through. Seizing hold of the old vine stem he swung himself across to the wall of Philemon's atrium, climbed over it and then swung down. He fell soundlessly and waited for a moment, crouching, listening. Something rustled, but perhaps it was the warm night wind. He got up and moved on stealthy feet towards his mistress' apartment. The curtain was drawn back, and a small rush light threw a black shadow on the wall. Someone was there.

Who could it be? The house was locked and the keys had been entrusted to Glaucus. Onesimus took a noiseless step forward and peeped round the edge of the curtain. At the same moment the breeze fanned the rush and the room was lit up. By the sudden light he could make out the figure of the bailiff crouched over a box, pulling out purple cloth and rich materials. The tiny flame flickered on gold bracelets and on the greedy, cunning face of the thief, and at that moment he glanced fearfully round and saw Onesimus.

Glaucus gave a stifled scream and stuffed everything

back in the box and slammed down the lid. The two stood facing each other in silence, breathing heavily. Both would have like to have murdered the other, but they had no weapons and were too evenly matched to try without. The bailiff realized that he had only one slender chance, and he risked it boldly.

"So!" he remarked, "I see we are both in this, so let us come to an agreement. We would both rather keep a whole skin and our master's confidence. Neither of us wishes to be branded. So let us agree to keep silence. You forget what you have seen, and I will do the same. Come, let us go quietly. The gate is open."

Onesimus stood considering. Philemon, being a Christian, was unlikely to brand and he himself had already survived several beatings and could survive a few more. He had little to lose, but the bailiff had everything.

The rush flickered and died, and they were suddenly plunged into darkness. Onesimus had a wild idea of flying at Glaucus' throat but decided against it. After all, a dead bailiff was no good to anyone; but a live bailiff in his power would be rather amusing and might even prove useful. It was a good bargain. Onesimus tiptoed out into the night and turned on his heel.

13

GLAUCUS AND ONESIMUS MET IN THE morning as though nothing had happened; but there was a noticeable change in the bailiff's behaviour. He treated the boy with a kind of frightened respect, and Onesimus rose when he liked and did what he pleased and did not do what did not please him. In fact he could have become very idle, had he not loved the spring work on the farm, the hunting for the ewes in the ditches, and the feeding of motherless lambs. There was no better place than the pastures on these warm April evenings when the flock wandered bleating toward the fold, and the daisies closed their petals and the sun went down over Laodicea. "What are you dreaming of, boy?" the shepherd would ask him as he stood gazing westward across the valley; but the boy would only laugh and pick up a lamb and fondle it in his arms.

But before the lambing was well over, a slave rode up to the farm on horseback and announced that Philemon and Apphia were already drawing near and were expected him by nightfall.

Onesimus did not question the slave about Archippus, because within a few hours he would see for himself. Ever since he had heard that there was a real possibility of healing, he had started to hope, and hope had grown to certainty, and he had not realized till today how shattered he would be if the miracle had not taken place, not so much for Archippus' sake as for his own. If Archippus were still lame, then never, as long as he lived, would he get rid of those feelings of guilt that sometimes tormented him on dark winter nights when the wind howled round the farm and bowed the trees like the clawing hands of some demon. But tonight he would be freed of the consequences of his sin. Tonight Archippus would walk in, and the torment would be gone for ever.

He did little that day, and Glaucus, ordering round the other slaves, was almost fawning in his politeness and consideration of Onesimus. Too restless to settle to any real work, he wandered off towards the canyons to pick a bunch of spring flowers for Pascasia's apartment, for the child loved flowers and would be weary after her journey. It was his last hour of idle freedom. Tomorrow Philemon would set him to work in good earnest, and he would be glad of it. He was tired of doing just as he pleased; and then he remembered that this was freedom! Just to do as you pleased for the rest of your life and to call no man your master! And he began to wonder, for the first time in his life, how much he would really enjoy it.

He turned at the foot of the canyon, as he always did, to watch the evening sun sink behind Hieropolis and bathe the walls and battlements in its last light. But as he did so, he noticed the small procession, headed by the carriage, climbing the hill toward the upper plain of Colosse.

Onesimus sped home. He could wait no longer to see what had happened. Would Archippus spring out of the carriage, or would he run the last lap, racing the horses as he used to love to do on cool evenings? Perhaps tomorrow he would climb the canyons. Yet just now they were trundling rather wearily up towards the farm, and there was no eager figure racing ahead. Probably he was waiting to give them all a surprise.

And then the carriage drew up, with the tired slaves toiling behind, and Glaucus the bailiff was bowing and scraping and rolling out pompous salutations. Philemon climbed out and lifted down his son, while Pascasia handed him his crutch; but there was no trace of disappointment on the boy's bright face as he greeted the assembled household. Pale with fatigue from the cramped hours in the carriage, he was smiling, and there was a look on his face that seemed like an expression of triumph.

Onesimus turned and fled!

He had supper with his mother that night. It was good to have her home, and she told him as much as she could about the morning they had spent with Paul. They had all gone out to Miletus, south of Ephesus, to meet the ship, and he came ashore and talked to them on the beach. Being a slave, she had stood at the back and had heard but little. Pascasia had never been on a beach before and had kept wandering off to find shells, and Nerissa had had hard work not to lose her. She did not really know what Paul had said - 'something about some wolves', she thought - but it was all very beautiful, and they had all knelt down at the end, and he had blessed them. Most people had wept because, with the dangers and persecutions he was facing, it was unlikely they would ever see him again. But Nerissa had not wept. To go to Christ and to rest for ever in His Home seemed to her the most wonderful thing that could happen to anyone. Her only fear was that her boy might not be there with her.

She was tired and slept early, but Onesimus lay awake till the fourth watch, tossing and cursing to himself. He felt he had been cheated. The dark shadow of his guilt would rest upon him for ever now, and he wondered what Eirene would say if she knew. But she must never know. There would always be a corner of his heart he could not show her. There would never be perfect truth between them.

For three days he managed to avoid meeting Archippus alone, or speaking to him, except for an embarrassed greeting, and he would have been surprised if he had known how much pain he was causing his young master. But on the fourth morning he was told to bring a sack of flour from the granary to the house, and, bowed under the weight of it, he lurched round the corner, not seeing where he was going.

"Stop, Onesimus! I can't get out of the way."

Archippus stood in the path, leaning heavily on his crutch, but he had called out too late. The top-heavy sack lunged forward and Onesimus with it, and Archippus went flying. The sack fell on the ground, and the slave stood stock-still, aghast, waiting for an explosion of rage. But it never came. Archippus' face was twisted with pain; but he recovered himself quickly and held out his hand.

"Please help me up, Onesimus," he said quietly. "It's a good thing I fell on that heap of straw. Hand me my crutch. It's all right; you need not look so frightened. It was not your fault, and I am not really hurt."

Onesimus gaped at him standing there pale and shaken

from his fall but completely in control of himself; and a sudden flood of compassion, remorse and admiration welled up in his heart. He was so overcome that he sat down on the flour sack and stared at Archippus as though he had never seen him before in his life.

"Master," he said slowly, his embarrassment forgotten, "I am really sorry you were not healed. What happened? I suppose all those miracles people talked about were just fakes."

Archippus lowered himself beside him with some difficulty, his pain forgotten. He had so longed for this moment, but now that it had come he felt unable to explain. Besides, sitting on a flour sack in the public courtyard was hardly the setting he had imagined. How could he make Onesimus see what he had seen? How could an unenlightened heart understand? How ridiculous it would sound! His slave would probably end up by despising him more than ever.

"No, they were not fakes; they were all true, and far more than we ever heard about..." he hesitated, and then plunged boldly on. "Paul talked to us all on the sea shore. He talked about the ministry he had received of the Lord Jesus, and about caring for the church; he called it the flock of God."

"Never mind about the church, Master," interrupted Onesimus. "They'll be out to look for this sack of flour. Tell me abut the miracle, or rather the lack of it."

"I went forward and spoke to Paul when it was over," went on Archippus steadily. "We walked along the beach a little way, and we sat on a rock and talked. I asked him to lay his hands on me and heal me, so that I could go with my father and Master Epaphras and preach the

Gospel all over Phrygia; but he said he did not think that was the ministry God had given me. He thought I was meant to stay and tend the church here in Colosse, like a shepherd feeds the sheep and guards them from wolves without; and I did not need to walk far for that. He said that the miracles were given as signs, but I did not need a sign. I must learn to walk by faith. And then he told me what had happened to him."

Someone with a loud voice, inside the house, began heaping abuse upon slaves who went to sleep in granaries. Neither boy took the slightest notice.

"He has a sickness he seldom talks about," went on Archippus, "and he is often in pain. Three times he prayed for healing, and the third time the Lord Himself spoke to him. He said, 'My grace is sufficient for thee, for my strength is made perfect in weakness'. And, do you know, Onesimus, ever since then he has been glad about his illness and weakness."

"Glad? Whatever for? You looked glad too, Master, when you were lifted out of that carriage. You Christians are strange people. I just cannot understand you. *Why* were you glad that day when you came home as lame as you went?"

"Because our weakness makes us lean so hard on His strength. Before I was lame I was so proud and strong, I thought I could do anything. Now I am lame, I know I can do nothing. My weakness leads me back and back to Him, and I love Him as a thirsty man loves the fountain and a cold man loves the fire. Only you cannot understand till you love Him."

"And you are content?"

"Not only content; I'm glad."

There was a light in his master's eyes that Onesimus had never seen before. He still did not understand, but he knew that Archippus had grown to patient, disciplined manhood, and in spite of his lameness Onesimus would never despise him again. For the first time in his life he gazed at him with respect.

"May the curses of all the gods descend upon you, idle slave!" shouted the cook flinging open the door of the house suddenly and throwing a bone which caught Onesimus full on the ear. "Am I to wait until..." Then he caught sight of the young master and retreated hastily, although no doubt he intended to finish his sentence in the kitchen.

Onesimus rose, helped Archippus to his feet, shouldered the sack and lurched ahead to get what he deserved from the cook. But Archippus struggled on over the rough ground till he found an outcrop of rock and sat down to rest. The spring sunshine warmed him; the golden faces of the dandelions smiled up at him; it seemed as though every bird in the canyon was singing to his happy heart. He looked out across the valley where his feet would never travel, to the mountains he would never climb, and he praised God.

He had won at last. Through all the years when he had sought so hard to impress Onesimus with his physical strength and beauty, his power and importance, his slave had hated and despised him. Now, his pride of life broken, a weak cripple with nothing left with which to impress, he had won his slave's allegiance. Perhaps, in time, he might even win his friendship.

14

TIME PASSED, AND THE BOYS GREW, THE ONE in strength and physical beauty, the other in maturity and wisdom. Archippus was now seventeen and would never attain his full height and would always drag his twisted body about with the help of a crutch. But during his father's frequent absences he had proved himself an able overseer of the farm and a kind, just master of men. His slaves loved and obeyed him and seldom took advantage of his weakness. But the one whose friendship he coveted above all others did not love him. Onesimus respected his young master and served him meticulously, but he never spoke to him unless he was obliged to do so and never remained in his presence a moment longer than was necessary.

"Onesimus," said Archippus one night, as his slave was clearing away the evening meal, "I am going to Laodicea tomorrow. Will you prepare my clothes for the journey?"

"Yes, Master," replied Onesimus. He carried away the vessels and returned and began to lay out the clean tunic and brush the sandals in silence, with the utmost deference. He had grown to manhood's height now, but still moved with the grace of an athletic boy, and Archippus sat watching him miserably. The beauty, the rippling muscles, the proud lifted head always woke in him an unconquered ache of longing, longing to be like him, longing to communicate. Two years had passed since they had sat side by side on the flour sack, but never again had the barrier been lifted. Onesimus was his slave, soft-footed, obedient, irreproachable in his duty; and beyond the mask of servility Archippus might never trespass.

"Would you have me attend on you, tomorrow, Sir?" Onesimus stood in front of him, hands clasped, head slightly bowed, a chattel, without an apparent desire of his own. Archippus could have screamed.

"Do you want to come?" he asked, in a voice half-pleading, half-exasperated.

"Your wishes are my wishes, Master," replied the boy automatically. He recognized the pleading and half enjoyed the game, for it gave him a strange sense of power; but tonight he wondered whether it was worth it. He would have given much to have gone to Laodicea. It was over two years since he had seen her... She would be a child no longer. He tried to imagine her taller, developed in figure, and he decided, with a rush of longing, to drop the mask. He looked up suddenly, but it was too late.

"Oh, very well," Archippus was saying wearily. "If it does not matter to you either way, you had better stay and help with the sheep-shearing. There is a gathering of the Christians in the church at Laodicea, and some of the Christian slaves will be coming with me in any case. I shall be meeting my father and Epaphras who are travelling down from Philadelphia tomorrow, and we will all return together. Be sure my father's apartment is ready before the evening. Goodnight." He turned away, and there was nothing for Onesimus to do but to reply respectfully and go.

Outside in the meadow he cursed himself bitterly for a proud fool, and he was half tempted to humble himself and creep back and kneel at his master's feet and ask to go with him. Although he had never asked anything of Archippus, he knew that he would deny him nothing. He hesitated, turned, and then turned back scowling. Was this how he wished to face her, meek, servile, in the background? A thousand times, No! He would go to her alone, walking as a free man with his head high, or he would not go at all. He picked up a boulder, sent it spinning towards the valley and cursed again. Then he went home and counted his hoard of coins. It had grown considerably heavier by now, and tomorrow, with Archippus and Philemon safely out of the house, it might even grow a little heavier still. He had been so careful, willing to go so slowly. And because he had never yet failed he had become so trusted.

He sheared the sheep and went about his other duties absent-mindedly next day, for his thoughts were with Archippus in Laodicea. What was he doing, he wondered. Probably he was singing those same old hymns in some airless inner chamber, wedged in with a lot of sweating slaves and fat Jews. However, perhaps not. The church at Laodicea was renowned for its prosperity and independence and seemed to have escaped any persecution so far; so perhaps they could hold their meetings comfortably and openly. He did not know, and he did not care, and he wondered, for the hundredth time, whether Archippus would see her. Probably not, as Polemon would hardly allow her to go near a Christian gathering, but one never knew. He suddenly wished he had gone after all, if only to have walked the streets where her little feet trod and to have looked on the scenes that her eyes saw daily.

The day drew on, and he saw them returning, far away and earlier than he had supposed possible, a tired little procession climbing between the green wheat fields, Archippus mounted on a horse and his father walking beside. These long rides on horseback always brought on attacks of pain, and Onesimus ran to the house to prepare his master's couch and fill the jugs with water and lay out clean clothing. He was just in time to reach the door and help Archippus alight.

"All is ready, Master," said Onesimus, helping to support the twisted figure which drooped with weariness. "Shall I help you to bathe and robe before your evening meal?"

"No, thank you," said Archippus. "Hand me my crutch and I'll see to myself. You need not wait, Onesimus. Goodnight."

With an effort he drew away, his face averted, and limped into the house alone, unnoticed by his parents who were busy greeting each other. His slave stood watching him for a moment and then shrugged his shoulders and turned away. "If he likes to struggle with jugs far too heavy for him, let him!" he muttered, but he was bitterly hurt and disappointed. He had missed his master more than he had realized and had been longing to hear what had happened at Laodicea.

He wandered moodily over to his hut, and his mother cooked his supper, but it did not cheer him. The very sight of his mother worried him these days. She had grown so thin and coughed so often, and sometimes he noticed her holding her side, her face puckered with suffering. She was often asleep when he came home at night, but she seemed restless in her dreams and often cried out as though in pain. Yet when he asked her about it, she would laugh and tell him that all was well.

"I am in Christ's hands," she would say simply. "Can any evil befall me?"

"Well, I suppose you can be taken sick and die in Christ's hands, the same as anywhere else, can't you?" he had answered rudely and gone off before she had time to reply.

He took a few mouthfuls of food, and then pushed the plate away and went out. He thought he would betake himself, and this demon of restlessness within him, to the canyons and climb until darkness fell. Even he strode across the upper meadow, the quietness and the scent of newly-mown hay soothed him, and he walked more slowly and then stood still. He sometimes imagined that on these long light summer evenings you could hear sounds too small for ordinary human ears; the rustling of the couch grass, the fall of the dew, the folding of the poppy petals, the flight of homing birds. His gaze came to rest on the shadowed town across the valley, where perhaps she was kneeling by some open window, robed for sleep, looking out on the evening sky. He wondered where her bedroom was, and whether she ever cupped her face in her hands and gazed over at Colosse. Then suddenly he was jerked back to reality by a sound that was not imaginary, but clear and very close at hand, the sound of a deep groan.

He peeped cautiously round the outcrop of rock from

135

behind which the sound came, curious, but unwilling to become involved in other people's troubles. But instead of seeing and creeping away, he stood rooted to the spot, pride and pity, fear, curiosity, all struggling for the mastery. For Archippus sat on the ground, his face hidden in his hands, weeping - Archippus who had never once, since his talk with Paul on the shore, spoken of his suffering or complained of his lot. Archippus, who for two years had shown a brave smiling face to the world, was sobbing like a child.

Onesimus stepped forward. He feared the light and peace that dwelt in Archippus, but here was darkness and conflict such as he himself knew. He laid his hand on his master's shoulder, and the boy started violently and looked up, angry and ashamed at having been discovered by his slave in this moment of weakness.

"Leave me!" he ordered; but Onesimus, for the first time in his life, openly disobeyed him. Archippus, looking up wonderingly into his eyes, saw, not the perfect, impersonal slave, but the boy he had grown up with gazing at him with deep concern and pity. Dashing the tears from his eyes, he pulled Onesimus down on to the grass beside him.

"What is the matter, Master?" asked Onesimus. "Did anything go wrong at Laodicea?"

Archippus gave a shamed little laugh and blew his nose hard. "Nothing but what I might have expected," he replied. "I've never told you, Onesimus; I never tell you anything, because you will not let me, but I have always loved her, ever since the day you found her in the canyons. Hardly a day has passed that I have not thought on her. In a way I knew; but in my dreams it is difficult to remember what an ugly weak creature I am. Only today she saw me for the first time since it happened, and now I know I need not dream any more."

"What did she say?"

"Oh, not much. She is still a child in some ways. I met her in the street, and she would have passed me by, only I dared to stop and greet her. When she recognized me she could not mask her horror and concern. She concealed it quickly and asked after my father and you, Onesimus, but she did not want to linger. She bade me farewell as soon as she decently could, and I know now that it is farewell for ever."

He spoke sadly and quietly, as though his passionate grief had died in the telling. They sat for a few minutes in silence, and then Archippus spoke again haltingly.

"I went on into the church. We started with a great love feast, food and drink in profusion. All seemed satisfied, patronizing, lukewarm, and I was like a man starving for living bread and water. Perhaps it was not Christ I was seeking. I wanted her, Onesimus, or, failing her, some human comfort and solace. He knew. He is very merciful toward our weakness."

"What do you mean, Master?"

"Oh, drop that 'Master' can't you? I loathe this master-slave relationship. We were babies together, Onesimus, and you were my friend years before you were my slave. And Christ was merciful. I needed Him, but He touched me with a human hand and spoke to me through human lips. You came..."

"Me!" repeated Onesimus, thoroughly alarmed at this new part he seemed to have played.

"Yes, you. You have not spoken to me like that for

two years, and I know now. Onesimus, why you put up these barriers and act like a dead dummy? Is it because I ill-treated you before I knew Christ? Heaven knows how I have repented of my pride and cruelty and deceit! Will you never forgive me?"

It was getting dark now, and a sickly moon had risen over the poplars. Deep called to deep, and truth to truth. "It's not that," said Onesimus. "I forgave you years ago. I think I am afraid of you. Or perhaps I am afraid of that Christ Who indwells you."

"Afraid of Christ?" Archippus sat up, his troubles forgotten, hope surging in his heart. "How can the dead fear life, or the blind fear light, or the lost sheep fear the Shepherd who comes to carry it home? Oh, Onesimus, if you only knew."

"I do know," said Onesimus hurriedly, "and I am still afraid."

"But of what?"

The slave sat silent. How could he tell Archippus how much he feared that light which would shine on his old sin and force him to confess it and cast it on Christ for ever? Far better to carry the guilty burden to the grave than that. And it would no doubt shine on that paltry heap of stolen coins and cut across his life's ambition. Far better remain in bondage to sin eternally than risk his chance of calling himself a free man in this world. He suddenly realized that he was desperately afraid now. Love was very near to him, in the tender colours of the sky and the breath of the warm summer night, in the strength and humility of the boy at his side, in the unrecognized Presence Who indwelt His people. Who could withstand that invasion and what would be the terrible consequences of yielding? He dared not even consider it, and he rose to his feet in panic.

"Come," he said harshly, "let us go home. That way is not for me, Archippus. I have told you before. I could never bring my life and plans into line with that sort of thing; but I am glad it is a comfort to you. You need it; I do not."

"You need it desperately," replied Archippus simply and then fell silent. Onesimus took his young master's arm and led him over the rough ground to the gate of the court where Apphia stood looking out over the dark fields, anxiously watching for her son's return. Onesimus bade him his usual respectful goodnight and turned home.

But his mind was in a turmoil. That night, what he feared had happened to him, as far as he knew, for the first time. According to the Christian jargon, of which he had heard enough to last him until he died, the risen Christ had drawn near to him and called to him, as surely as He had drawn near to Archippus when he fell under the feet of the mob. But the price He asked was too high, and Onesimus had made his great refusal. Now let him weigh up his assets and live for them alone, for they were all he had.

He drew out his bag of coins and went over and stared down at his mother. She was asleep, breathing very rapidly and tossing restlessly. He shook her gently, and she woke with a start.

"Mother," he began, sitting down beside her, "do you remember that night when we sat in the doorway at sunset and you told me all about my father?"

She lifted her white face to his, and a little flicker

of fear passed over it, but she answered quietly, "I remember, my son."

"Mother, do you remember what else you told me that night?"

"Yes, I remember." She shivered and started coughing.

"Mother, I want to see that little hoard of coins. I want to count them. The time may be very short now, and I must know what is mine."

So he had never guessed, and she must tell him. "They were not yours, my son," she said. "They belonged to my mistress. When I turned to Christ He bade me put away stealing and restore to every man his goods; so I returned them. How could I do otherwise when He called me to walk in the light?"

Onesimus clenched his fists. He was alone, forsaken. They had all gone over to this Jesus, and even his own mother had betrayed him. In his fury, he struck out at her in the dark. She fell backwards with a little gasp and started coughing again.

Terrible choking coughing! Thoroughly alarmed and bitterly ashamed, he lit a rush and brought her water and helped her to sit up. And as he did so, he saw that her pillow and gown were spattered with blood.

15

NEXT MORNING ONESIMUS WENT UP TO THE house and told Apphia that his mother was ill and too weak to rise. Apphia was not surprised, for she had known for a long time that her dear slave was dying.

Nerissa did not rise from her bed again. The hut was small and airless, and Apphia wanted to carry her over to her own cool home, and care for her there with her own hands; but Nerissa refused to leave her son. So Apphia visited her two or three times a day and nursed her tenderly, and when Onesimus came home from work he often found them talking together. And they talked, like pilgrims about to set out on some happy journey, of their beautiful destination and of the Loved One who awaited them.

Onesimus went about his duties in an agony of sorrow and remorse, and at night he would sit late beside his mother and tend her himself. Neither had ever mentioned the blow he had given her; but one evening when he was pouring spring water over her hot hands, his wretchedness was so acute that it cried out to her without words, and she pushed aside the basin and took his hand in both of hers.

"Do not grieve, my son," she said. "I know how you felt and how heavy is the burden of your slavery; and when Christ finds you, you will know, too, why I acted as I did. It was not the blow you dealt me that made me so ill. I have been sick for a long time, and I have known that I should soon fall asleep in Jesus. And oh, my son, how glad I should be to go if it were not that I fear to say goodbye to you for ever."

He clung to her, weeping like a little boy. He had not really realized until now that she was dying.

"Mother, will you forgive me?"

"Peace, my son! My life is already in Christ, and I shall go Home; but you are more to me than life, and how shall I rejoice if you are not coming?"

She sank back exhausted and soon fell into a feverish sleep. But he lay beside her for a long time, sorrowing and wondering and afraid. His blow had made no impression on her love for him; indeed she scarcely seemed to remember it. If human love could be so unquenchable and forgetful of injury, what of that divine love? Perhaps, after all, he could not cast it off as easily as he had imagined.

The end came quite soon. A soft summer rain was falling, and she woke suddenly just before dawn.

"What is that noise?" she asked.

"The rain," answered Onesimus. "It is a good thing the hay is in."

"I thought it was the sound of footsteps running to meet me," she said. "The gate is open and I know now Who it was that Stephen saw. But I turned and looked back, and I saw you following hard after in the way, so now I can enter in peace, and you, my son..."

A violent fit of coughing cut her short and after that she lay very still. Onesimus sat beside her until he could see her face by the first pale light. Then he knew what had happened, and he ran to waken Apphia.

They robed her in white and buried her in the earth, according to the new custom of the Christians. Nobody sorrowed greatly, for they would very soon see her again, and the hymns they sang were full of praise for the glory and rest they would all soon share. Only Onesimus sobbed out his very heart alone in the canyons and wished he could die, yet he feared to die.

But he turned a stony expression to the world and hurt Archipppus intolerably by the way he kept him and his sympathy at arm's length. Only the pain in Onesimus' eyes and the whiteness of his face could not be hidden, and Apphia and Philemon spoke of it one night in their bedroom. "That poor boy," said Apphia, "I half fear for his reason. He looks as though he will never smile again."

"I know," answered Philemon. "He will not accept the comfort we have in Christ, but a change might do him good. The shearing is finished and in two days' time I am sending Glaucus to Laodicea with the last bale of wool. He must bring back the money and will need a trusty bodyguard. The boy can go with him."

Onesimus received the news without any show of pleasure, but his spirits lifted a little. If he could see her and tell her about his mother, he thought he would find some comfort. It was most unlikely that he would see her; for the warehouse was in the middle of the city and her house on the outskirts, and Glaucus would no doubt keep a sharp eye on him. Still, he was young and hopeful, and nothing was impossible.

Onesimus was up before dawn on the great day, dressed with special care, and he had the beast laden before Glaucus appeared, bleary and blinking and

143

grumbling. He waddled behind the horse and Onesimus strode in front, leading the way into the lower valley. It was strange, sultry weather, and no birds sang in the poplars. The hot mist seemed to rise from the fields, and clouds lay low on the mountains. Thunder rumbled round the valley.

"The gods must be angry with us," remarked Onesimus. "I expect there will be a real downpour on the way home."

He said this purely to annoy Glaucus who had an unholy fear of offending his own Christian God, and he enjoyed the look of distress on the bailiff's face. Glaucus was old and fat and hated a wetting but he never dared reprove Onesimus for anything he said, for from that day to this each had guarded the other's secret.

They paused for a hasty meal outside the city, but not for long, for the weather was getting more and more strange. The sky was a smoke red, like some weird, lost sunset, although it was only after midday. The streets were almost empty, for the air in the city was oppressive and most people were indoors taking a siesta. Glaucus, panting and perspiring and glancing at the sky, was very unhappy indeed.

"Go and have a rest, Master Bailiff," said Onesimus. "Do your business with Master Polemon, and then spread out the bale in the warehouse courtyard and have a sleep. I will wander about the city for an hour or so and come back in time to reach home before dark. The evenings are long and light and there is no need to hurry."

"This evening will not be as other evenings," said the old man nervously. "No, no, stay beside me, young man, and let us start home as soon as we possibly can. This is sick, unhealthy weather, and I fear a storm."

They reached the warehouse just in time, for Polemon was about to go home for dinner. He greeted them somewhat contemptuously, for he thought anyone connected with Philemon the Christian must be a fool. But in money matters Glaucus was no fool, and he watched keenly as the wool was weighed and the payment was calculated and counted and re-counted. But at last they were all out in the street bowing farewell to each other, Glaucus impatient to be off, Onesimus frantically seeking some excuse to stay

And it was then they felt the first tremor.

It was a small one, but they all knew what it meant. Earthquakes were common in the Lycus valley. Already white-faced people were pouring out from the doors of the houses and the voices of women screaming for their children were heard within. And on all lips was the same cry, "Make for the open spaces! Make for the market! Keep clear of the houses!"

Glaucus fled. It was amazing that anyone so old and fat could run so fast. Onesimus seized the horse's bridle and dragged him whinnying toward the centre of the market. Polemon stood hesitating in an agony of indecision.

And then came the second, stronger tremor. The big houses shuddered and righted themselves. Two or three of the smaller ones fell in like a pack of cards. Onesimus turned to see whether Polemon was following and saw him dash back into the warehouse, crying out like a man possessed, "My gold! My gold! Oh ye gods, spare my gold!"

Then came the third, last mighty tremor and the whole

145

city seemed to collapse with a rumble and crash around the fugitives in the market square. The warehouse had suddenly disappeared, and in its place stood a great heap of stone and brick. Onesimus shuddered as he thought of Master Polemon lying far below the stone and plaster, clutching his gold with dead hands. But his mind was concerned neither with Polemon nor with Glaucus, trembling and gasping in the middle of the market, nor with his own safety. The big houses on the circumference of the town were less damaged than those in the centre, and she might well be safe. But whether she was above ground or under the rubble, he must reach her at once. His own life was of little account; in fact his heart leapt at the thought of laying it down for her sake. He slipped the horse's halter over a post and struck out for the Hierapolis gate.

He knew the way well, for he had trodden it so often in imagination; but even so it was hard going. Whole streets were blocked, and people knelt in the rubble, weeping and calling on the gods as they scrabbled with their hands. In places great pillars swayed unsteadily, and the townsfolk were swarming to the gates to take refuge in the meadows and hills.

Over the heaps of stone, brick, plaster and dust, over great slabs of marble, through crowds of dazed men and women and crying children, Onesimus fought his way to the house on the hill. He could see from some distance away that the roof had fallen in, but the walls were still standing. He strode in at the gate, and she ran straight to him and clung to him.

"My father! My father!" she cried. "Where is he? Have you seen him, and is he safe?"

He looked down at her ashen face, her hair and dress still white with plaster, a great bruise swelling up on her forehead, and he could not tell her the truth at once.

"Has the warehouse fallen?"

"I believe that most of the houses in the centre fell."

She gave a groan and covered her face with her hands.

"Mistress Eirene, there may be yet another tremor. The people are flocking to the gates. It is better that we go. If you like, I will take you back with me to Colosse, and Mistress Apphia will care for you."

She shook her head.

"No, no," she cried. "My father may yet come and I must wait for him. They will dig in the ruins, and whether dead or alive, I must see him again."

"But you must wait outside the gates. Where is your governess?"

"I have had no governess this past year. The slaves all ran away as fast as they could. Take me to Euphron's hut, Onesimus. He is my father's shepherd, and his wife will take me in. There is no one else."

Her natural control was coming back to her, and she had ceased to cling to him. Despite her unkempt appearance, she stood there like some lonely little queen, facing her fate with dignity. His heart ached to take her in his arms and comfort her, but he dared not presume on her plight. Never before had his slavery seemed such an insuperable obstacle.

"Come, Eirene," he said gently, taking her hand, for her eyes were still fixed on the cratered road to the town, and she lingered. "We must go now, at once. I will take you to your shepherd and his wife and leave you there in safety; but there is no time to lose. One more tremor and the gate may fall."

She came at once, and he led her out into the street, drawing her on through the crowds. Most of the people were heading for Hierapolis or Colosse, and some of them, too exhausted to travel, or wounded, were planning to camp by the river. Euphron's wattle hut was off the beaten track in a small grove of trees. It was a peaceful place surrounded by lawns of wild flowers where the sheep grazed. The tremors had barely shaken the hidden valley, but Euphron and his wife, Antonia, were already climbing the slopes toward the town, and Eirene, letting go of Onesimus' hand, ran straight into the old woman's arms, weeping.

"My father!" she sobbed. "The warehouse has fallen, and I think he is dead!"

"Then you shall come with me, little Mistress, and be our daughter until the day when we can restore you to your inheritance. See, I will take you back to our home where you can rest, and Euphron, you go on to the town and seek further news of Master Polemon, and wherever you find homeless or motherless little ones, bring them here, and we will shelter them for Christ's sake."

She turned back and led Eirene into the hut. It was clean and cool and strewn with rushes, and Antonia laid her on a straw pallet and brought her milk and bathed her bruise and comforted her as one comforts a little lost child. Then, as the old woman turned, she noticed Onesimus lingering in the doorway. She looked at Eirene questioningly, and as she did so she traced a swift sign with her finger on the pillow, and Eirene almost imperceptibly shook her head.

"Come in, boy," said Antonia kindly. "Sit and rest awhile and tell us more of the disaster. You yourself look white and shaken. Are you a citizen of Laodicea, and has your home fallen?"

Onesimus sat down in the doorway and told them all he knew, except that Polemon had died trying to rescue his gold. He had not the heart to tell them that; it would come to light soon enough.

And now, what next? There was nothing to stay for. Eirene was safe, and Euphron would soon return with a collection of howling waifs and orphans. Antonia has gone to the well to fetch fresh water, and he and Eirene were alone.

"Well, I had better go," he said, rising; and going over to the pallet where she lay, he gave her his hand and the old greeting: "Goodbye, little Mistress Eirene; we shall meet again"

She looked up, arrested, and a faint colour tinged her white cheeks. He had come to her and stood by her like a rock in the storm, and she suddenly realized that when the ceiling had crashed on her and she had fled out alone into the garden and found herself forsaken, she had known he would come; and having found him, she had known she was safe. She wanted him to stay for ever, but she was fourteen now, and it would be unmaidenly to say so.

So she just held his hand in both hers and said, "Thank you, Onesimus... I... I knew you would come... and... we shall meet again."

He let go her hand and stumbled out into the early evening, his blood thundering and his eyes smarting, and a mighty resolve growing in his heart. So! She had known that he would come. She had not forgotten. In her terror and fear of death she had remembered him and known that he would come. Now nothing should stand in his way. He would go away, now, tonight, and never return until he could walk through the gates of Laodicea as a free man and claim her.

The city was strangely quiet apart from the pitiful little groups tearing at the stones and rubble with bleeding hands, while slaves dug frantically beside them. The lower streets were partly flooded by fountains and sewers, and a sour smell hung over everything. Onesimus found Glaucus and the horse still standing in the middle of the market, as the old man had been too afraid to move. He was very angry with Onesimus, but as usual he dared not show it.

"Come, come," cried Glaucus, his teeth still chattering so that he could hardly speak. "It is high time we started for Colosse. The night will overtake us before we reach the upper plain. Where have you been, Onesimus?"

"Never mind where I have been," replied the boy. "Hoist yourself up on to the horse, and we will go." He lifted the old man into the saddle and led the frightened horse over the ruins to the southern Syrian Gate. They were halfway down the hill to the highway when he suddenly jerked on the bridle and drew the horse behind a screen of cypress trees.

"Glaucus," he said in a tone of authority he had never used before, "hand over that money in your wallet."

The old man's eyes nearly started out of his head, and his face turned a muddy yellow.

"The money, Onesimus? Our master's money? Are you mad?"

"No, not mad, just in a hurry. Hand it over, Glaucus. If you refuse, I shall go straight to our master on our return and tell him all I know. You have always hated me; now is your chance to get rid of me. Go home alone and tell Philemon that Polemon and I and the gold perished under the warehouse."

The frightened bailiff made one more attempt.

"I, too, have my secret, Onesimus. If you tell of me, I shall tell of you. For the love of God, end this foolish talk and take me home."

"Glaucus," said the boy, "hand over that money or I shall strangle you. I care not what you tell of me, for I have nothing to lose. Christians do not brand, and as for the rods, I tasted them when I was young and weak, and I can stand them again without flinching. I care not a straw for my reputation. But you, Glaucus, do you relish being beaten by some low menial and your stewardship being taken away from you? And what about your comfortable, honoured old age? And what about your cosy seat in the church? Think twice, Glaucus."

He needed no further persuasion. Slobbering and trembling, the old man flung the packet of gold on the ground and turned the horse's head.

"Go, thief, villain," he shouted, with a most un-Christian-like curse. "And may you never come back again."

"That will depend on how well you can persuade them that it is useless to search for me," replied Onesimus. He skipped down the hill and turned his back on Colosse. The open highway and the wide world lay before him.

16

HIS FIRST THRILL OF ELATION WAS followed by a wave of fear. He had never realized till now how much that he had taken for granted had been thrown in with his slavery: a roof over his head, a bed, food, clothing, regular work, and, he had to admit, a kind, just master. Now he had forfeited his right to these things for ever. From now onward he must fight for them and earn them or go without. He was glad he was not alone on the highway. He was just one of a stream of nameless refugees, some of whom purposed to push on to Ephesus or Miletus, while others would seek shelter in the towns and villages along the highway. Some had snatched up a few possessions, and some came empty-handed. No one spoke to anyone else. All had their own griefs and problems, and, shocked and stunned, their one idea was to move on, they knew not where.

The sultry day was fading early, and the storm clouds hung low, blotting out the mountains. Very soon darkness would draw a veil over the stricken city, and Onesimus knew that it would be a moonless, starless night, and he was glad of that too. He must push on as fast as he could, for he did not entirely trust Glaucus. It was just possible that the bailiff, out of spite, would decide to behave like a genuine Christian and confess his sins and those of Onesimus as well. In that case, they would soon be after him on swift horses with hunting dogs, and he would not stand a chance. Tired as he was, he resolved to walk all night and sleep hidden away in the hills by day.

It was an inky night. Only the black shapes of the trees on either side kept his feet on the highway, but he walked on, hungry, weary and cold, until about four hours after midnight. All the other travellers had fallen behind, and his head was reeling and his feet were blistered, when he realized that something was happening. A cock crowed, some birds twittered and the cattle in the fields stirred in their sleep. A small wind, sweet with the scent of hay, was rustling in the poplars, and now he could see the shapes of the mountains, black against a clear sky. He scrambled up the bank into a spinney of larches and found a hollow sheltered by some tamarisk bushes. He turned and looked toward Colosse and Laodicea and saw that the day was breaking behind his own mountains and canyons. She would be asleep now in the wattle hut, worn out by her grief, and on the other side of the valley Archippus was probably lying awake, his leg aching as usual, mourning for his slave and friend. "I'm sorry, Archippus," he whispered, and creeping under the tamarisk bushes, fell asleep with a strangely heavy heart.

He slept all through the warm summer day and awoke an hour or two before sunset with a raging hunger. It was good to know that he could buy bread. He fingered the packet of gold tucked into his wallet and the small bag of coins sewn into his girdle. Something had prompted him to bring it with him when he set out for Laodicea. The highways abounded with robbers, and he must sew the gold into his clothing as soon as possible, although his tunic was so plastered with earth and dust that most people would mistake him for a beggar.

He travelled twenty-five miles that night, and on the fourth day trudged over the shoulder of Mount Coressus and saw the town of Ephesus below, lovely in the evening light. Memories came flocking back: the horror of the temple, that nightmare evening when Archippus fell, those strange unearthly nights when they huddled in Aquila's house. He wondered where that queer fellow Paul was now - probably murdered long ago.

He would have loved to linger, but he dared not. His master had many friends in Ephesus, and he might easily be recognized. He struck straight down to the canal and followed it to the harbour. If his luck held, he might get a ship. He would not argue about where it was going as long as he could put the sea between himself and the country of Phrygia, but his longing was to reach the land of his father.

Several ships rode at anchor, and he stood looking westward. Over the edge of the harbour, somewhere beyond the sunset, lay Athens and Parnassus where the gods dwelt. If he could get to that shrine of beauty and worship there, would he perhaps find what he was seeking: some balm for the sorrows of life, some escape from its sordidness, some philosophy that would lull him, rather than challenge him, and cause him to forget rather than stab him to remembrance? Perhaps beauty was the answer. Then he would search for beauty.

One Mediterranean galley, larger than the rest, had just been loaded and the sailors were walking away. But a boy of about Onesimus' age lingered, walking the length of the craft and back again, as though examining it closely. He was meticulously dressed in a spotless tunic and the long wide-sleeved overcoat of the educated Greek with a rich ornamented strip of material sewn down each side. His features were pure Greek and his figure that of a young Spartan athlete. He seemed to Onesimus to embody the land of his fathers, and he watched him, fascinated, for a time. Then, acutely conscious of his own condition, Onesimus dared to ask him whether he knew whereto the ship was bound and when it would sail.

The boy looked at him disdainfully. "It is bound for Corinth but stops at Athens," he replied in perfect Greek, "and if the wind is favourable it should sail at dawn tomorrow."

He was turning away when Onesimus tried again.

"I want to travel on her," he said boldly. "To whom should I apply?"

The boy raised his eyebrows. "It costs money, you know," he said.

Onesimus flushed angrily, and his pride overcame his prudence. "I can pay my fare," he replied hotly.

"Well then, perhaps you had better first pay the price of a new tunic," said the boy. "This is a first-class ship and, if you do not mind my saying so, you hardly look a first-class passenger."

Onesimus' temper was getting the better of him. "I suppose you have hardly heard of the disaster in Laodicea," he retorted sarcastically. "Hundreds are dead in the earthquake and we who fled did not think it worthwhile to go back and search in the ruins for our banquet clothes. We were thankful to escape with our lives, and extra thankful to escape with something in our wallets."

The contempt had passed from the boy's face and he looked at Onesimus with interest. "The Captain is already on board," he said in a different tone of voice. "Come before dawn and speak with him."

Onesimus turned on his heel and followed the harbour wall round to the beaches and plunged into the warm sea. It was nearly dark and he washed away all the dust and dirt of the past four days and then tried to do the same for his clothes. He dressed again in soaking garments, and afraid of soiling them by lying down, he wandered about on the beach till after midnight when the summer wind had dried him. He slept for a few hours on a slab of marble and just before dawn he was back on the quay. The sea was still dark, but the sunrise flamed over Mount Coressus, and the quay in front of the galley was a hive of activity, for the wind was favourable. Sailors ran to and fro, ropes creaked, men shouted, and a little apart stood the Captain, with the young Greek beside him, a well-filled wallet over his shoulder.

"This is the lad of whom I spoke," said the Greek. "He lost all, or nearly all, in the Laodicean earthquake; so make a merciful bargain with him. He wants to go to Athens."

How does he know I want to go to Athens, thought Onesimus, drawing out the little packet from his belt as the Captain named a price. He was relieved that it was no more, and he counted out the coins gratefully. There was still plenty.

"You can go aboard now," said the Captain and Onesimus passed up the gangway onto the galley. He had never before set foot on a ship, and it thrilled him. This was a merchant ship, taking the products of Asia to

157

Greece: sandals and woven cloth, cloaks and carpets from Laodicea, Phrygian embroidery, cheese from Bithynia, figs from the central plains behind Ephesus, goatskins and wool from the Cilician grasslands. A rich medley of odours, heightened by the tang of the sea, rose from the hold. All at once bells started ringing, the sailors ran to hoist the great central sail and the ship heeled away from the wind and they were off. Onesimus staggered to the side of the ship and saw the bright sea ahead. Phrygia and his slavery lay behind him at last.

But not only Phrygia and his slavery. He stood saying an irrevocable goodbye to Philemon, Apphia, Archippus, little Pascasia, the dogs, his mother's grave, the canyons, the flowered meadows, the flocks of sheep. So much that he had hated and so much, too, that he had loved! But he did not say goodbye to little Mistress Eirene, for he had pledged himself to see her again.

His musings were suddenly interrupted by the Greek boy who had come to stand beside him.

"My name is Alpheus," said the youth. "I see we are travelling to Athens together. Have your ever been before?"

"Never," replied Onesimus.

"Are you a Greek?"

"On my father's side."

"Then you are returning to the land of your fathers and to the home of your spirit, if you love beauty and truth; And I see from your face that you love beauty. You must come with me. Nothing could give me greater joy than to initiate a young devotee of beauty. I will stand beside you as we sight the Cape and see the white temple of Poseidon; and then we will watch together the flash of Athena's spear above the Acropolis. We will climb the steps of the Parthenon..."

"And how does one earn one's living in Athens?" Onesimus was half irritated, half fascinated by his companion.

Alpheus looked pained as though Onesimus had said something vulgar, and his reply was unsatisfactory. Apparently you did not earn your living in Athens. You were sustained by beauty, and the spirit dominated the body. You talked and worshipped and meditated. Sometimes you wandered out on to the fragrant slopes of Hymettus and lay on beds of thyme and tasted the honey that was like nectar of the gods. Onesimus, fast yielding to the fascination, remembered that he still had plenty of gold in his wallet and gave himself up to the spell of the moment: the light roll of the ship, the swelling white sail against the azure sky, the smooth peacock blue of the Aegean sea, the warm salt breeze and the pure clear-cut voice of the boy.

He was talking of the history of his country now. One evening in the cool they would walk out together to the plain of Thermopylae. One day they would rise at dawn and climb the slopes of Mount Parnassus. The magical voice crooned on, telling enchanted tales of an enchanted land, and Onesimus stretched out in the sun, and slept peacefully.

The enchantment did not break when, on a pale golden evening three days later, the western light gleamed on Athena's spear, and the pillars of the Parthenon against a rosy sky seemed themselves tinged with pink, as though newly alight from heaven.

Alpheus stood in the prow of the ship, his beautiful

head lifted in silent adoration, tears in his eyes, and Onesimus shared his mood. They watched till the light faded, and as the stars shone out over the city the ship cast anchor in the Bay of Phaleron.

They went ashore early next morning and set out to walk the five miles inland along the wall of Themistocles, and by the time they reached the city the heat was blazing. Young Athens for the most part laughed and studied and discussed history and philosophy in the shade of trellised vines and marble pillars. Onesimus was grateful to find himself completely undertaken for by Alpheus who treated him with princely generosity. He produced a clean tunic for him from somewhere and introduced him to a group of his friends. They had all feasted together on bread and goats' cheese and melons and slept in the shade. In the late afternoon they joined a crowd of disputers in the lovely theatre of Dionysius at the foot of the Acropolis; but Alpheus insisted they should not climb the hill until the evening.

"When the world is still and the light is mellow," he explained, "and the pillars are like warm gold. That is our moment. Not in the glare of noonday, but the mystery of twilight we will worship our goddess. Oh, Onesimus, have you ever yearned for beauty and peace and truth? Tonight you will be satisfied."

It was the time of clear golden light when they finally climbed the steps of the Acropolis and passed through the Propylaea. Through the great marble pillars the sea shone like a sheet of silver, but inside the great temple of Athena it was already shadowy, and Onesimus, keyed up to highest expectation, was not disappointed; for here was beauty incarnate, some quality of perfect simplicity such as dwelt in the soul of the little Eirene. Here was no taint of occult evil as in the temple of Ephesus. Here he was standing on the very fringes of immortality. As they knelt, worshipping, before the mighty statue of Athena he felt strangely close to the boy at his side. To come together to the source of beauty and wisdom and to share these emotions was surely the firmest basis for friendship, and from now onward they would be brothers. Life could never be quite the same again.

They stayed for a long time beside the statue. The golden light flamed to sunset, lighting up the golds and crimsons of the temple. They wandered all over it and round the precincts, looking up to the shadowed hills and over to the darkening sea. Onesimus' soul, awed by the solemn chanting of the priests and virgins, was drunk with such beauty, but his heart cried out, "What next?" Could he carry it with him when he returned to the world below where men ate and slept and spat and cursed and hated and lied, where slaves groaned and earthquakes destroyed and the innocent suffered? Was there any meeting point? Had any god come down in compassion to men? Had Athena ever stooped to heal and transform with her beauty and her wisdom? He did not know. He must discuss it with Alpheus.

"Come, let us drink to the goddess!" Alpheus led him outside, and they sat down on a hillock below the temple. Although Alpheus had implied that, having seen the temple, they would be in no further need of earthly food, Onesimus was relieved to see that he had brought a full basket of provisions. The warm night was heavy with the scent of thyme and mint, and Alpheus, his beautiful features clear cut against the moonlight, filled two cups with wine from a bottle.

"We will drink and watch the temple washed silver by the huntress, Diana," he jested, handing Onesimus a cup. "To the goddesses!"

The slave was tired and thirsty. He drank it off in one draught. It was very sweet and strangely strong. "Alpheus," he began, turning to his friend, but Alpheus sat looking out to sea, his wine untouched in his hand.

"Alpheus!" Something was happening. The boy at his side seemed to be receding, and the marble columns away to his right were reeling. He closed his eyes and laid his head on a pillow of wild thyme and seemed to be sinking down, down into its fragrance. Had the goddess stooped, taken him into her arms? He did not know, but he gave himself up to deep sleep.

Alpheus emptied his glass on the ground. He glanced at the sleeping boy contemptuously. "Poor fool," he murmured. It had all been too easy! He had a good meal from the basket and then prodded Onesimus with his foot. He did not stir; so there was nothing to wait for. Leaning over, Alpheus loosened his companion's girdle, slit out the bag of coins and the packet of gold with his knife, hid them under the contents of the basket and bounded off down the hill.

17

WHEN ONESIMUS REGAINED CONSCIOUSNESS next morning, he could not imagine where he was. He was still under the influence of the drug, and the noise of the city below seemed hundreds of miles away. The sun burned down upon him, and his head was aching and so heavy that he seemed unable to lift it. His mouth was parched and he was sweating profusely. Water! Shade! Oh, where was he? And what had happened? His hand strayed to his girdle and he found it undone. He knew something had gone, but he could not remember what. If only there was some water and some shade! He dragged himself up the hill and into the shade of a great marble pillar, and little by little it all came back to him. He opened his eyes with difficulty and caught sight of the crimson skirts of Athena's robes.

So! He had been deceived, betrayed and robbed, and this was the other side of beauty's gilded coin! Suddenly the temple and all that it stood for seemed desecrated and meaningless, and he rose dizzily to his feet. He was able to stagger to a fountain and dashed the water all over his face and head and drink deeply, and then, flinging himself face downward behind a clump of cypresses he wept weakly for bitterness of heart and utter disillusionment.

But he dared not lie there for long; for there was a pressing problem to be faced. He was alone in a strange city without food or shelter or a single sestertius to his name. He could trust no one and expect mercy from none. However ill he felt, he must find work quickly.

He was suddenly very sick, and after having washed his hands and face again he felt better and found he could walk down the Acropolis. In the streets of the city the rich young men lounged and disputed as usual, and the Parthenon in its unearthly beauty dominated Athens, etched against a hot blue sky; but for Onesimus the glory had departed for ever. There was no meeting point. Let the gods remain in their marble halls and temples, and he in future would remain with his feet on the ground in this cruel, treacherous world.

He could not walk far, but he found a little shade behind a column and dozed for a time. A kind old fruit seller gave him a bunch of sour grapes about noon and he ate them gratefully and asked where he could find work. She looked him over thoughtfully.

"The young men of Greece like to work with their tongues and their brains," she replied with a smile. "But they say there is money in the ports for any who will work with their muscles. You look strong and broad-shouldered. You should go to Piraeus or to Corinth."

He thank her and made up his mind immediately. As soon as the day began to cool he would start and walk all night. He must get right away from Athens. It would take him about ten hours to reach Corinth, perhaps longer with a splitting head and an empty stomach; but in any case he would start.

He set out just before sunset, glad of the sea breeze on the westward highway. It was a quiet evening, and he was thankful to shake off the dust of the city and plunge into the waters of the Bay. As he passed through the little town of Eleusis the moon rose, and he glanced with a shudder at the great covered Hall of the Mysteries. It was nearly time for the Eleusinian celebrations and rites, and he had hoped to see the torch-bearing procession. But now he had had enough of mysteries and temples! All he asked of life was food in his stomach and money in his purse.

The road to Corinth soon wound up into the hills, and the olive trees and vineyards, flooded by the full moon, gleamed silver. He helped himself to bunches of early grapes and broke through into a garden and picked a handful of figs. They were refreshing but not sustaining, and when at last the road dropped down to the shores of the Gulf of Aegina, weariness overcame him and he lay down and slept on the warm sand. It was evening again before he had trudged footsore and hungry into Corinth. He had spent a few hours in the afternoon working in a vineyard and had earned the price of a meagre supper. Worn out, he curled up in an old archway and slept fitfully on its marble base.

The first light woke him, and he rose, cold and stiff, and made his way to the port, a two mile walk along the forty-two feet wide Lechaeum road, descending by steps to the harbour. In front of him lay a forest of masts, hiding the waters of the Gulf - all the great merchant fleets of Italy and Spain, of Africa and Asia, loading or unloading their goods, setting out in a favourable wind, or being wafted into port. The streets seemed thronged with merchants of every race: Romans, Greeks, Jews, Syrians and Egyptians. Unlike the citizens of Athens, all seemed in a hurry and bent on business, their one link their love of money. Onesimus gazed into the tired, crafty faces and felt he had come home.

He had little difficulty in finding work. A squad of loaders belonging to a ship bound for Brundisium had mutinied over their wages, and the sailing had had to be delayed. The owner of the ship took one look at Onesimus' broad back and rippling muscles and employed him for the day. He found himself one of a gang of young Corinthians, and all through the hot morning hours he unloaded great bales of merchandise and helped clean the hold. At midday he joined the other workers for the welcome ration of food in the shade of the warehouse, and he listened, fascinated, to their conversation. These were real men of the world, the first he had ever met at close quarters. He longed to grow up and become one of their company.

They spoke chiefly in veiled language, barely understood by Onesimus at first, of their experiences in the groves of the great shining temple of Aphrodite, the goddess of love, set high on the tawny mountains that dominated the city, the Acro-Corinth. They spoke of this temple without reverence or emotion but with a kind of fierce excitement. As they drank their wine the unseemly jests grew freer, until they spoke without shame or restraint and boasted of the orgies in which they would take part that night. It was full moon. Some festival was taking place and the goddess of love would provide free pleasure for all.

Only one boy sat apart and did not join the jests and conversation, and for some reason Onesimus' eyes kept wandering back to this boy's face. This was strange; for apart from his fine physique he was not a good-looking boy. But there was a grave aloof expression on his face, and his eyes seemed to be looking far away. He reminded Onesimus of somebody, but the likeness eluded him. The boy ate his portion of beans and barley bread like the rest, but when they lifted their wine cups and drank in the name of Aphrodite, Onesimus noticed that he quietly laid down his cup and looked away.

They worked all through the blazing afternoon and lined up for their pay at sundown. Already the lights were twinkling in the city as they turned up the highway from the harbour, and men were thronging to the groves on the slopes of the mountain, their faces wild with excitement.

"Why don't you come home with me?" said a quiet voice at his side. "You are a stranger, as I heard you telling that fellow when we rested. You can sup and sleep at my home tonight."

Onesimus turned, surprised. The boy who had sat apart was standing at the crossroads in the shadow of Apollo's temple. The crowd was surging forward, and the young slave was following them eagerly. His whole body tingled with excitement. This was surely life, this was pleasure, this was what men meant by love. And yet, looking into the eyes of the boy, Onesimus suddenly knew of whom he had been reminded. The aloof gravity, those deep brown eyes, that simple way of speaking. There was some quality in him akin to Eirene. The thought of her arrested him, and a great wave of homesick longing and shame swept over him as he realized that he had forgotten her as he followed the mob. There was no room for her image in these wild revellings that took place in the name of the goddess of love.

Besides, he was desperately hungry, and the temple on the hill promised no food. He hesitated for a moment and then turned and followed the boy down a side street that led to the potters' quarters in the city. The coolness of the night restored his reason. He had been drugged, he had walked forty miles, slept little and worked all day in the blazing heat. He had been crazy to think that he could have rushed up that mountain. All he wanted in the world was food and drink and a pillow on which to lay his still aching head.

It was comparatively quiet in this part of the city. They had left the broad crowded streets and the taverns where Syrians, Greeks and Romans drank and brawled. They walked in silence, both a little embarrassed at this sudden gesture of friendship, until they reached a small house beside a pottery dump and Nestor, the youth, went in.

The family were at home, and Nestor gave his father the usual kiss of greeting. "Father," he said, "I have brought a friend home for the night. He is a stranger in Corinth and has nowhere, as yet, to go."

"You did well, my son," said his father. "He is welcome." Then he glanced at Onesimus, and, picking up a piece of charcoal from the brazier, he sketched a quick sign on the floor. Nestor shook his head. It was over in two or three seconds, and their guest was drawn in and made to sit down. A little girl brought water for his hands and feet, while Nestor went off to bathe and change into a clean tunic. But while they were busy setting the meal, Onesimus stared hard at that rough mark on the floor. It looked as much like a fish as anything else. Then a good meal of meat was brought in. All the family gathered round, and the father of the family blessed it in the name of Christ.

Christians! That was what was the matter with them all! Onesimus had sensed a difference from the beginning. There was an indefinable atmosphere about the place, just as there was in Philemon's home. He thought he had escaped from Christ and His people, but here he had tumbled right into the middle of them again. Well, there was nothing to do now but enjoy the meal and the kindly company. The mother was asking him where he came from, and all seemed anxious to help him. Even the smallest sister was picking out the best fruit for him. She was a tiny fragile little maid of about four years old, with smooth brown hair that rippled to her waist. He smiled at her and found himself wondering what Eirene would have looked like at four years old. She would have felt at home here. He relaxed and told them that he was a Phrygian nobleman who had lost his family and his estate in the Laodicean earthquake.

Wine was passed round, the schoolboy brother recited his lessons, and they talked of the Christian church at Corinth. It numbered many people, both men and women. There was to be some kind of gathering tonight and Nestor and his father were going to it. They invited Onesimus to come too; but he was giddy with sleep, so they made up a bed for him in the pottery shed, blessed him in the name of Christ and left him.

He must have slept for a couple of hours when he was wakened by low voices. Father and son were sitting on the step enjoying the moonlight and the night breeze. Drowsily he listened to their talk.

"How are you getting on at the port, Nestor?"

"Quite well. It is not easy, though. They cry out the

name of a god over every bottle of wine they open. And their talk! Must we always live in Corinth, Father? It is like living in a sewer. I don't wonder our young men are drawn away. That lad tonight - he is only young - I should imagine from the practised way he works that he is a runaway slave, and he was following them up to those vile groves hardly knowing where he was going. That is why I asked him to come home with me."

"You did well, my son, and in the morning preach Christ to him. But about your work: I shall soon be able to buy my own potteries and take you on as an apprentice. But in the meantime remember what Paul wrote in his letter to us. He said that to get away from fornicators and idolaters you will have to go out of this world. Learn to live among them, remembering that our body is the temple of the Holy Ghost, bought with a price..."

Their voices trailed on, and Onesimus fell asleep again. He was not anxious because they had guessed who he was; for these men would not betray him.

After breakfasting together in the morning the two lads set out early for the harbour, and as they sauntered through the quiet streets the shyness that had been between them was somehow broken down.

"No need to hurry," said Nestor. "The others will all of them have been dead drunk and will not be able to stand on their feet for another hour or two. We shall not start work yet."

Onesimus eyed him curiously. Now that he had slept off his weariness, he half wished he had joined the revellers the night before, just to see what happened.

"Have you been up there, Nestor?" he asked abruptly.

The young man smiled rather sadly. "Many, many a time, Onesimus," he answered. "I was just like the rest were until Christ found me. We all were. Even when Paul preached Christ to us, we did not really understand. We had been brought up in this sewer. It was not till he wrote us a letter that I really abandoned it completely. He told us our bodies were members of Christ, temples of the Holy Spirit, washed, justified, sanctified. It was difficult at first; but now I even hate to hear them talking about it."

Onesimus stared at him in amazement. "Are you really speaking the truth, Nestor?" he blurted out suddenly. "Are you a man with red blood in your veins, or does your Christ turn you into a puppet, or into some sort of god? I just cannot understand it."

Nestor stood still to consider his answer. He was not offended; he was searching for the right words.

"I think I am more of a man now than I ever was before," he replied thoughtfully. "I was just a beast before, obeying every desire of my body, yet with part of me, the spirit God gave me, hating it but powerless to stop it. Then . . . yes, I suppose you might say that in a sense we became gods. Paul said that God shined in our hearts and we saw the light of the glory of God in the face of Jesus Christ. God in Christ, Christ in us, and so we became real men with power over our lusts and our sins, new creatures in Christ Jesus. Would we want to go back to being beasts? Old things are passed away, and all is become new. God came down to us in Christ."

They had reached the harbour road now and walked in silence. Nestor's bright face lifted to the morning. Onesimus suddenly gave a little start. This was the question he had meant to ask Alpheus, and here was the answer. It could not have been put more plainly. God had come down to him in Christ and was, it seemed, pursuing him in Christ. There *was* a meeting place; but he had spoken the truth that night when he had sat in the hayfield with Archippus and said, "I am afraid of the Christ that indwells you."

He was more afraid now. He felt as though immortal Feet were following him. Everything had failed him. Diana was a hideous idol; in the fair temple of Athena he had been betrayed and robbed; in the courts of the goddess of love there was neither tenderness nor purity, only shame and lust and filth. Christ, with His terrible demands, was the only One left.

He must get away from these Christians, for they savoured of Christ. His wages were in his pocket, and he would eat, drink and be merry. They had nearly reached the port now, and he looked up and saw a proud ship with an unfurled sail riding on the morning swell.

"It must have cast anchor in the night," said Onesimus.

"Just for twelve hours," replied Nestor, who knew the ways of ships. "That is the Emperor's corn ship. If the wind is favourable it will sail tonight for Puteoli or for Ostia, the port for Rome."

And Onesimus, with the impulse for flight strong upon him, said to himself, "And I will sail with it."

18

"DO YOU WANT A JOB?" ONESIMUS started. He had been sitting half asleep in the spring sunshine on a crate on the edge of the Forum. It was seldom possible to sleep much in Rome because of the noise of the populace by day, and the noise of the vehicles at night, to say nothing of the bitter cold of winter and the raging heat of summer. But for a few weeks it would be spring and the snow would melt on the Alban hills. In the gardens along the banks of the Tiber the grass would be green, and flowers would bloom in spite of the crowd and the stench of the sewers. He had been half dreaming there on his crate. Spring in Colosse! The swollen torrents, the clean air from the heights, the blessed, blessed silence broken only by the crying of the lambs, the narcissi along the water courses! Oh, ye gods! Why had he ever left it?

"Do you want a job?" The voice was peremptory and impatient.

He lifted his head and look at the speaker with blurred eyes. His face was thin and haggard, the face of a weary man; but he had worked as a drawer of water, and it had kept his muscles in good trim. The man in front of him seemed to be staring at his muscles and measuring his broad shoulders as though he might do something with them.

"What sort of a job?"

Anything would be better than his present life, and only the night before, terrified by the collapse of a crazy top-heavy building in the street where he lived, he had half decided to slip down to the river and make an end of it all. The Tiber was the common grave of thousands who could face life no longer. But the water was filthy, and he feared death. Better to go on for a while. Things could not always be as bad as this. Perhaps with the coming of the spring his luck would turn.

"A good job," said the man, "a job for a man with muscles, and a chance to rise to fame and glory and riches. A chance to reach the Imperial court and to stand before the Emperor himself! What about it? Come and train as a gladiator. Nero's marriage to the divine Poppaea will take place shortly and the games must be more brilliant, more daring than ever before."

Onesimus looked at him thoughtfully and then gave a little laugh. "And a chance to die with a dagger through my belly, my head in the sand," he retorted. "However, death is probably better than the life I lead now. Do you house and lodge me ?"

"Everything," replied the man. "Fetch your goods and report to me this evening. You will take your oath and belong to the first gladiatorial troupe in Italy."

He turned away, and Onesimus rose and walked slowly through the streets, his brain numb. Down the stinking, airless little alley, where no breath of spring could ever come and where the dregs of the population huddled in constant fear of fire and collapsing masonry, he made his way to the tall four-storeyed house where he had his home in an attic under the roof, with little ventilation and less light, where vermin blackened the walls at night and where he slept fitfully on a shelf of masonry sticking out from the wall.

He had little to collect: a small bundle containing a change of clothing and a few sesterces and a blanket he had saved up to buy. He tied them round him and went to inform the landlord that the attic was now vacant. Then he was out in the street with a free day ahead of him, before he sold himself irrevocably, body and soul, into the keeping of the procurer, into a slavery that could be ended only by death or by the bestowal of the wooden sword that signified repeated victory.

How should he spend his last day of freedom? He would eat bountifully tonight; so he exchanged his few coins for some bread and fruit and wine and trudged out of the city. On he went, past the Circus, under the arch of Drusus where he turned to gaze at the great Imperial palace on the Palatine, on through the rows of suburban villas and the jostling crowds of peasants bringing their country produce into market, until at last he was out on the Appian Way, with the Alban hills lying in the cool morning sunshine to his left. Slipping between the tombs and statues that lined the road, he followed a little pathway up into the hills and breakfasted on a slope near a foaming stream. The grass all round him was starred with marigolds and daisies. Birds sang and young lambs bleated, and just below him in the valley an orchard foamed with peach blossom. Nearby, a happy slave sang as he dug an irrigation trench, and a child laughed beside him. Everything heralded a fair new beginning, but Onesimus knew that for him it was the end.

Two years ago, footsore and hungry, he had walked

the hundred and forty miles from Puteoli to Rome and stood for the first time on the crest of the Appian Way and looked down, thrilled, on the vast densely populated capital. Here was the heart of the Empire, the seat of the god-Emperor, the land where the nations of the earth poured in their corn and their wine, their spices and merchandise, the city whose legions tramped to the farthest corners of the world. Surely here he would come into his own and find his freedom and lift up his head among men. Here, somewhere amongst these marble temples and glittering statues, he would find his fortune, and then he would hasten back over land and ocean, proud and free, to Laodicea.

He had quickly discovered that Rome had two faces. In neither of them had he seen any good thing as yet. The golden god-like Emperor, whom he had once seen reciting his own poems in a public theatre, was a fat, hysterical and loose-mouthed young man, who, it was whispered, had murdered his mother and his wife and banished his wisest counsellor, Seneca. All over Rome slaves described his night orgies, where men and women ate until they vomited, and then ate again; where wine flowed in fountains and the guests drank until they fell under the table. The face of the court was corrupt, cruel, pleasure-loving, fantastically luxurious.

And the other face was the face of poverty. Thousands, who were supported by the free corn that the Emperor issued, spent their lives idling and watching the games; but the strangers, the wretched riff-raff who, like himself, had left their own countries and had been lured to Rome by its fair promises, were not eligible for the corn ration. Huddled in dens and in tottering, vastly overcrowded houses, they sought what living they could or, starving, sold themselves back into slavery.

Yes, that was what it had all come to. The struggles of the past two years had ended in this, a new and sinister slavery with the almost certain prospect of a violent death, in exchange for food by which to prolong the ghastly business of living.

He wandered on for a long time, far into the heart of the hills, breathing deeply the warm spring air, drinking from the unpolluted springs, looking perhaps for the last time on greenness and flowers, and trying not to remember. In the afternoon he turned back to the city and before sunset he had taken his oath and signed. He had hired himself body and soul, abandoning all human rights, to march at the command of the procurer. The enormous meal which was served up as soon as he entered the barracks cheered him, for he had not seen a meal like this since he left Colosse. Wine flowed freely, and the apartments where they were to live were comfortable, with baths and gymnasia. Perhaps as long as life lasted, it would be enjoyable, thought Onesimus; and then he looked round at his companions, and his heart sank. They were men with enormous frames and bulging muscles, giant-like men in full training, but their faces were coarse and brutalized with the shedding of blood, and many of them boasted scars. Most of them ate gluttonously and jested and swore. There was to be no tournament tomorrow, and all they had to do was to enjoy themselves.

But not all were like that. Over in the corner sat a man unlike any whom Onesimus had seen before, a fair-haired, blue-eyed giant who ate with restraint. He neither jested nor swore, and his face, as he looked round on the company was very sad. Once his eyes rested on the boy, and he smiled a gentle half-apologetic smile.

But if the food and lodging were of the best, the training school was proportionately brutal. They were treated with the harshness of convicts, flogged and inflamed like animals. Sweating, panting and cursing, they were daily driven through superhuman tests of strength and endurance and mercilessly punished if they failed. By the end of the fourth day Onesimus, lying exhausted on his back, wondered bitterly what real difference there was between them and the wild beasts in the cages in the amphitheatre, whipped, snarling, into learning tricks for the Emperor's amusements.

Opening his eyes, he was surprised to see the blue-eyed gladiator sitting beside him. "Tomorrow is a festival," he said, speaking slowly with a foreign accent. "Nero will sit on the Emperor's throne in the amphitheatre, and we will fight in couples to the death. You will be taken to watch and to become hardened to the sight of blood."

Onesimus paled. "And you?" he asked. "Will you fight?"

"Yes. I have fought twice before. I struck down my opponent and won the palm. If I can win three or four times more they will give me my rudis, and I shall be free of this vile, murderous business for ever."

"But, if you hate it so, why did you sign on?"

"I had no choice. I was brought over from Britain in the triumphal march of Aulus Plautius. Many of us were killed; but I was only a young boy, and he took me for his household slave. For seven years I served him and his gentle wife Pomponia Graecina, and then she was tried by order of this evil murderer, the Emperor, because she served other gods than those which all Rome has discarded. Her household was broken up and I was sold to a cruel, idle master. He died from drunkenness and carousing and I, because of my great strength, was sold to the procurer."

"And if you gain your rudis, what will you do?"

He smiled his gentle smile that made him more of a stranger than ever in this coarse, violent company. "Who gains his rudis becomes a rich man," he said. "First I shall buy my freedom, and then, when the next legions march, I shall go home."

"Home? To Britain?"

"Yes, it is a good land. No scorching heavens and no screaming hideous cities. The earth is red and rich for ploughing. The seas are cold and grey, and purple heather rises from the rocks to meet a grey sky. Our wattle hut was close to the shore. Maybe it still stands."

"Whom will you fight?"

"I do not know. We cast lots for our partners. Look well at your comrades tonight, Onesimus. Only half of them will return. The blunt and padded weapons with which you learned to thrust and lunge will all be discarded tomorrow and exchanged for swords and daggers of sharpened steel."

A lavish banquet had been prepared for the gladiators that night, and the public was admitted to view the heroes of the morrow. Most of the gladiators gorged and jested, for if their hours on earth were few, let them enjoy what remained. Some ate sparingly and drank little for fear of dulling their senses; and some, the fear and shadow of death already fallen upon them, wept and called on the gods.

To Onesimus it was a ghastly and sinister meal, and he had little appetite. He managed to sit near the Briton and drew strength from the older man's sad calm. He had cared for no one for so long; but now he suddenly found himself longing passionately that his friend should win and be free and go back to his strange cold northern land, to his fathers and his gods.

"What gods do you worship in the land of Britain?" asked Onesimus suddenly.

The man turned thoughtfully.

"In my country we worshipped the gods of thunder and war, and to them I cry in the arena. But my Mistress, Pomponia, worshipped a God of mercy and peace and love, who called all men to Him, Jew and Gentile, bond and free, male and female, the grown man and the little child. If I die tomorrow, I commit my spirit to the God of Pomponia."

Onesimus stared, and the colour drained away from his face. Again? Were those tireless Feet once again catching up on him? They must surely be the same - no other god had called Himself the God of mercy and peace and love. The years rolled back, and he forgot the belching and sucking and loud laughter going on all round him in defiance of death. He seemed to smell sweet herbs hot in the sunshine, to see a fair face lifted to his, framed in flowers, and to hear a voice say shyly, "Did any of our own gods say, 'Let the little children come to me'? I think only Christ said that."

19

THE BRITON WON HIS PALM AND HIS training became more rigorous, but throughout the scorching summer months he was kept back from the amphitheatre. Nero's marriage with Poppaea was drawing near, and the most promising gladiators must not be killed before the great days of feasting and holiday. Onesimus, too, on account of his graceful body and good looks, was being carefully protected from death or scarring. Daily he fought with blunt weapons and developed his muscles in the gymnasium. To accustom him to the sight of blood he was forced to go twice a week at dawn and witness condemned criminals thrown to the wild beasts, and twice, at a real celebration, he had been paired with a semi-trained gladiator who showed no promise, and he had struck him down easily with a sharp blade. The first time he had trembled and sickened, but the second time he had turned away quickly from the crumpled form in the sand and received his palm, fixing his mind resolutely on the gold and silver pieces showered upon him by the onlookers.

He was daily becoming more and more inured to the carnage and bloodshed, and more akin to the hardened brutes around; but two threads held him back from utter vileness and degradation. One was his friendship with the Briton, who seemed incapable of contamination and who hated the whole business from start to finish. This man, amid death, violence and debauchery, remained his gentle child-like self, in the company but not of it, his goodness the rock to which Onesimus clung lest he lose his humanity and become a beast for ever.

The second thread was the memory of Eirene. He dwelt in the scorching city where the sand reeked of dried blood and men sank lower every day. But her country was the canyon where the air was cold and clean, the water pure, and the rocks sharp and rugged. If he were ever to meet her again, he must not sink to the status of a beast. If he went on winning, he might one day become a rich free man. Like the Briton, some day he might even go home.

As the burning, thirsty days passed, the training of this picked group of winners became more specialised. They no longer fought in the amphitheatre but rose at dawn for their first exercises and ate apart on a diet of special quality. Their massage took longer, their tournament practice became more intense, their leisure more carefully supervised. 'Cattle primed for slaughter' their companions called them, but Onesimus was beginning to enjoy himself. All those who survived the great days of the wedding festival would almost certainly receive their rudis at the end, and he could not help knowing that the betting on the winners was almost all on himself and the Briton.

Now that the days for the festivities drew near, the group was seldom allowed beyond the barracks, for they were reckoned about the most valuable property in Rome; but even they could not miss the sense of excitement and the frantic preparations that were being made. The praetorian cohorts of the Campus Martius were drilling in squadrons nearby all day long except for their noon siesta, and the harbours were thronged with ships bringing choice fruits, spices and gold and silver curios from the ends of the earth. Every country sent its tributes to the Emperor, and the menageries were being lavishly replenished. Night after night, great cages were wheeled through the streets bearing hippopotami from Nubia, lions from Mesopotamia, elephants, tigers, leopards and panthers from North Africa. Sleep, in certain quarters, became impossible because of their anguished roaring. Everyone was in high holiday mood, for corn and wine and sweetmeats would be showered upon the populace, and all would live to the full for a few glorious weeks.

Onesimus, as the opening day drew near, was in a restless mood. By day he exulted, scenting the blood of battle, hearing the clash of arms, sure of victory. If he came through this orgy he would certainly receive his rudis and rank with some of the greatest names in Rome. But at night he would wake with strange fearful forebodings, breaking out in perspiration as though the shadow of death already hung over him. One night it was so terrible that he rose and paced the floor of his dormitory, and his friend, the Briton, came and paced beside him.

"I know," he said. "This is the terror by night. I do not think I shall ever see my country again. Oh, what would I not give to feel the soft summer rain on my face and smell the wet loam of the oak woods."

But the first few days of the festival went well. The Briton was in the Samnite group and fought with sword and shield. Onesimus, in the Thracian group, was armed with a dagger and a buckler, and the two carried all before them. Day after day, when the other entertainments had taken place and the satiated crowd sank back exhausted, they alighted with the other gladiators from their carriages, and new life came to the amphitheatre. They marched round the arena in military costume followed by servants who carried their arms. When they reached the royal box, they turned and extended their right hands to Nero and addressed him: "Hail, Emperor, we, about to die, salute thee." Day after day they saw their opponents sink down, sometimes dead, sometimes wounded. If strength remained, the loser would lift his left arm in an appeal for mercy, and in that deathly silence all eyes would turn to Nero who could save life or pass the death sentence with a flick of his thumb. Day by day they received costly rewards, dishes laden with gold and precious gifts. They were becoming rich men, and surely it could not be long now before they were liberated. So many had died.

Then the blow fell. It had been a tremendous day. The charioteer and their racehorses had given a thrilling performance and covered themselves in glory. Twenty elephants had fought to the death with a team of armed barbarians. Criminals had fought with leopards. Elephants had traced Latin phrases in the sand with their trunks, kneeling before the Emperor's box. Armed men had fought with bulls, and lions and tigers had torn each other to pieces. And now the jaded spectators, tired of violence, death and blood shedding, wilted in the sultry evening.

Food, gifts and purses were showered upon the crowd, for enthusiasm must be kept at fever heat.

Poppaea, sitting beside her husband, was seen to yawn, and something must be done quickly. Nero whispered to a valet who sped off on an errand.

"The gladiators, the gladiators!" It was the cry that usually brought everyone to attention; but tonight Rome languished. The applause was less deafening than usual as the young giants saluted their Emperor and went back to draw for their partners. They found the procurer looking thoroughly perturbed.

"The divine Emperor desires a novelty," he announced. "He has commanded the Briton to fight the Phrygian, Thracian against Samnite, dagger against sword. It will be an ill-matched fight. Take your arms. The music is striking up."

So it had come to this. Friend must kill friend. Onesimus averted his eyes and then found that his mouth was dry with fear. The Briton would win the rudis today, for the sword would triumph easily over the dagger, but he, Onesimus, would not be there to rejoice.

"Hurry!" hissed the procurer. "The trumpets are blowing."

There was a gasp of surprise as the two winners with their rival arms entered the arena, and then roar upon roar of deafening cheers. No need to stimulate the crowd now. Even the Senate had half risen from their stone seats. There was a silent moment of agony, and then the Briton lunged half-heartedly with his sword and Onesimus deftly dodged and pricked his opponent with the dagger.

What was happening? These men were playing for a truce, not fighting to kill! Nero would lose his temper in a moment and the crowd was screaming to inflame them. The instructor crossed the arena, whip in hand, and began to thrash them on the calves of their legs. "Strike! Slay!" he hissed. "Are you women that you dawdle like this? Strike! Slay! Or I will turn the beasts on you!"

The Briton gave a tremendous lunge, but it was only the flat of his sword that came down on Onesimus' left arm, cracking the bone like matchwood. The boy's buckler fell to the ground and he sprang close. Shutting his eyes he plunged the dagger deep into the flesh of the Briton who gave a last blind thrust into Onesimus' shoulder and staggered backwards, bleeding. He was sinking down, and the screaming, crazy triumphant crowd had risen to their feet to a man.

Onesimus drew out his dagger from his opponent's breast. He had followed his instincts and pierced him just above the heart. He heard nothing of the savage yelling. He was standing looking down, alone with his pain and his dying friend who could so easily have killed him if he would. The blue eyes looked straight at him again, and there was neither anger or resentment in the look, only the same patient sorrow and kindness. "To Pomponia's God of mercy," he whispered, and then crumpled into the stained sand. The Briton had gone home.

"The rudis! The rudis!"

The words were taken up in a swelling roar all round the amphitheatre. Nero was leaning forward from his box, his bloated face creased into a snarling smile as he dropped the coveted wooden sword, the sign of a gladiator's release. Gold, flowers, gifts were falling round him, but Onesimus turned his back on them all and fled from the arena. He was gasping from loss of blood and in agony from his fracture, but this was nothing compared with the agony of his heart. What were riches and fame and glory now? He had killed his friend, the one in whom dwelt the only good that he knew in this vile city. Then let them die together!

He was out in the dark streets, and a full moon was shining down on him, and it was blessedly cool. The Tiber was not far off, and he would walk along its bank a little way to where the water was less polluted, and then - he hoped it would be oblivion, but he was not sure. There had been a way to eternal joy, but he had long ago refused it. He was conscious of eyes watching him as he dragged his feet along the road: the wild eyes of Archippus as he fell beneath the crowd; the loving eyes of his mother when he dealt her that blow; Glaucus' frightened eyes as he flung down the gold; the sorrowful, forgiving, dying eyes of the Briton. Haunted, conscience-stricken, wretched, he staggered on, and now he stood by the black waters of the river, the fear of death enveloping him, and he hesitated, irresolute.

Footsteps on the path beside him! He turned, startled, as a figure passed by him, unseeing. But the moonlight shone on the strong Jewish features and Onesimus knew them instantly. The years rolled away and he was back in the weaving shed at Ephesus, a tired boy who thought Philemon would never stop talking.

"Master Aquila! Master Aquila!" He was down on his knees in his stained finery clutching the man's cloak with his right hand. Then the moonlight darkened, and the murmur of the river ceased as he fell in a dead faint upon the ground.

20

HE WAS CONSCIOUS OF BEING LIFTED AND carried somewhere, of agonizing jolting, of the murmur of voices, of sudden peace and silence, and then he knew nothing more until the following day, when he awoke to find the afternoon sun making golden patterns on a courtyard covered over with vine trellis. He himself was lying on a couch in a little room opening off the yard. Being very weak from loss of blood, he lay for a long time motionless, slowly remembering all that had happened. His stained purple and gold uniform had been removed, and he had been washed and clothed in a cool, white linen robe. He was glad that all the blood had been washed away. His arm had been skilfully set and splinted and tied across his chest, and the wound in his shoulder was staunched and dressed.

Into what peaceful human paradise had he fallen? His last clear memory was the darkness and the black waters of the Tiber in whose foul depths he would have been lying now if it not been for that face. He could not remember clinging to him as to an anchor, but he was sure that through the mists of horror he had caught sight of the face of Master Aquila of Ephesus. He supposed it must have been he who had brought him here and staunched his bleeding and saved his life.

But did he want his life to be saved? Other memories came back in full force: his friend lying limp on the dark sand; the vile attendant, disguised as Charon, hastening up to strike him on his head with a mallet to ensure that he was really dead; that last gentle look of forgiveness, and the whispered words of peace. Onesimus turned his face to the wall so that none might see his wretchedness.

He heard a light footfall in the courtyard, and he looked up. A woman was standing gazing down at him, and he had seen her face before. In just this way she had stood looking down on him on that terrible night when he had thought Archippus was dead, and she had comforted him and fed him.

"Mistress Priscilla!" he whispered, wondering whether perhaps after all he had taken leave of his senses and was seeing ghosts.

She went on staring down at him as though she, too, recognised his face and was trying to remember where they had met. But the memory eluded her, and she shook her head.

"Ephesus," said Onesimus in a weary voice. "You sheltered me and put me to sleep with your little Levi on the night that Paul the Jew left the city."

"I remember." Her face was thoughtful. "You were a poor frightened child then, looking for your master. You have greatly changed. How do you come to be in Rome?"

He had not thought out any plausible story, but realised that he was singularly free from fear, for these Christians would not betray him behind his back.

"My master set me free," he lied, "I worked my way to Rome on a corn ship and won glory in the amphitheatre."

"So you were wounded fighting. I recognised the dress of the gladiator. You had bled much. You are fortunate to be still alive."

"I would I were dead," he blurted out. "Mistress Priscilla, last night I killed my friend. What is life or glory to me now?"

"There is forgiveness and new life," she said gently. "But you must rest now, and then one of the elders of the church will talk with you. See, I have brought you a potion to ease your pain, and Master Luke, the physician who set your bone and staunched your wound, said he would look in before sunset."

She gave him a soothing drink and arranged his pillow and went away to prepare a meal. The pattern on the floor got brighter and then faded altogether as the sun sank behind the tall buildings. Then the outer door opened, and the physician who had attended him came in and examined him carefully and redressed his wound.

"You look better," said Master Luke: "But your arm was badly broken and you lost much blood. You must rest for a time."

Onesimus looked up troubled. "Did Master Aquila bring me to his home?" he asked.

Luke hesitated. This young man with the sin-seared, weary face had won in the games. His rudis lay on the ground beside him, and he would probably be consorting with men of high station as soon as he recovered. Already the first rumbles that were to end in the great tempest of persecution were making themselves heard. Some of their group had already been tried and sentenced; Paul was in prison. It would not do to give anyone away. He replied diplomatically.

"Did you know Master Aquila before?"

"Yes, I knew him when I was a boy back in Ephesus. Last night he passed me in the street. I was in deep trouble, and it was good to see one face that I knew. I called out to him in my weakness and sickness, and then I knew no more. It was good of him to bring me here."

"Yes, Mistress Priscilla is a woman full of good works who has nursed men who were homeless and needy. I understand you have met her before too."

"Yes, also in Ephesus. How strange it is! During these two years in Rome I have seen no kind face and found no good thing save in one, and him I killed with my own hands in the arena last night. And now it seems as though chance or the gods have brought me to those who care for me. Life is cheap in Rome. Why was I not left to die in the street or to cast myself into the Tiber as I purposed? It would have been better for me."

"But you say you knew Master Aquila and Mistress Priscilla. Would you have expected them to leave you to die in the streets?"

"No, because they worship their God, Christ, and He enjoins them to be merciful. It seems to me that you, too, Master Luke, worship Christ, for you have doctored me well and made no bargain as to fees. But I can pay you what I owe, and Mistress Priscilla too. Up at the barracks my reward waits for me; only last night I had no heart for it."

Luke did not seem interested.

"Then you have heard of Christ?"

"Many times. Priscilla will tell you I am a freed slave. My master was a Christian and all his household."

"Then do us this favour, which is better than gold. When you return to fame and great riches do not betray this house nor those who come here. Some of them you may meet daily in Caesar's palace. Do not recognise them. The times are hard for those who follow Christ, and the Emperor frowns upon us. Remember that you received good, and forget this home."

"You are safe. I have no taste to return to the great and famous. I am sickened with bloodshed and pleasure and drunkenness and hate."

"Then stay with us and learn of Christ." There was a pause, and Onesimus was silent. Luke rose, for his patient's eyes were bright with fever.

"I will see you again on the morrow," he said. "Farewell."

But he did not leave the house. He crossed over to a room opening out of the courtyard and soon Mistress Priscilla appeared with strengthening food and wine; and Levi, who was now a fine boy of twelve, stayed and helped him eat. His father, Aquila, had not yet come home.

But Onesimus could not sleep. For one thing, something was happening in the house. Every few minutes the outer door opened softly, and Onesimus could see the dark forms of men, women and children crowding into a room on the far side of the atrium. He could hear anxious whispering and the voice of Luke the physician reasoning with them. By the light of a tiny lamp the sick boy could see them huddled together, their shadows thrown grotesquely on the floor of the courtyard. The lamp stood on a table and there was a cup and bread. Suddenly their voices rose in a hymn, and Onesimus lifted his head and strained his ears to listen. Clear and sweet through the darkness the words reached him:

"Jesus Christ came into the world to save sinners. If we die with Him, we shall also reign with Him."

Sinners! What a sinner he had been! What treachery, what lies, what hatred! It was too late now, for he had long ago spurned Jesus Christ and fled from Him.

The voices droned on, one after the other. He could not catch what they were saying and he dozed a little. Then suddenly he woke, for someone was concluding a reading, and his voice rang out, strong and vibrant, through the little house:

"For I am persuaded, that neither death, nor life, nor angels, nor principalities, nor powers, nor things present, nor things to come, nor height, nor depth, nor any other creature, shall be able to separate us from the love of God, which is in Christ   Jesus our Lord."

And maybe not distance either, not land nor sea, thought Onesimus with a little shudder. He had fled thousands of furlongs from the voice of that love, and yet he could not get away from it. Could it be that those swift, terrible Feet were pursuing him even now and had nearly caught up with him? Must he soon turn and face this God of love?

When Aquila came tip-toeing in later to settle him for the night, he found his patient trembling and drenched in perspiration.

"What is that book you were reading?" asked Onesimus abruptly when they had greeted each other.

"We read from the letter Paul wrote us four years ago," replied Aquila. "We had just returned from Ephesus when it arrived. The little church had only learned of Christ by those who had heard of Him from others; and when things are passed from mouth to mouth they become confused. He wrote to explain just why Christ died; but we still had many questions. It was a great day for us when Paul arrived in Rome."

Onesimus, in spite of his weakness, half sat up. "Paul!" he repeated. "In Rome! You do not mean to say he is here now?"

"Why yes," replied Aquila, "he has been here for over a year. He was brought as a prisoner because he appealed to Caesar. But they treat him quite kindly. He lives in his own hired house and is allowed to receive guests and to write his letters. Only of course he is chained day and night to a guard, so there is no privacy."

But Onesimus was not listening. "I must go and see him," he said.

21

ONESIMUS GREW STRONGER RAPIDLY, AND after four or five days he told Luke, his kindly physician, that he felt he should be moving on and not presume on Mistress Priscilla's hospitality any longer. His money was in safe deposit up at the barracks, and he would pay for his lodging and find other quarters. But first he had a favour to ask. Would Luke take him to visit Paul?

Luke was surprised. He had sat daily with this unhappy boy and had spoken to him of Christ, but he had made no response, only moved his head restlessly on the pillow as though reluctant to hear. He did not know that Onesimus was haunted day and night by a burden of guilt that had suddenly become intolerable and yet, glimpsing the price he would have to pay to get rid of it, hardly dared face up to it.

"We will go tomorrow," said Luke, "in the cool of the day. He is imprisoned near the Praetorian barracks."

They set out together next evening, Onesimus feeble as an old man and leaning on Luke's arm. Aquila lived in the Jewish quarter on the far side of the Tiber, so they crossed the river together and rested in one of the gardens on the bank. They went on slowly, and about sunset they reached the small house they had come to seek in the shadow of the barracks.

"He has many, many visitors," said Luke, "You may have to wait before he can give you an audience."

He knocked at the door and a voice bade him enter.

"Is it Luke?" said the tired voice of an old man within. "I am glad you have come. We have a singular joy this evening. Who do you think has arrived to visit us, all the way from Phrygia?"

Phrygia? Onesimus would have fled, but curiosity kept him rooted to the spot. Luke drew him gently in, and when his eyes became accustomed to the gloom he saw a sight he would never forget.

A man, round-shouldered and small in stature, sat on a stool chained by his wrist to a burly Roman guard who lay full length on the floor, fast asleep. The prisoner was the same Paul he had seen at Ephesus, but infinitely older and frailer, and he peered at the newcomers with dim scarred eyes, as though he had difficulty in recognising them. Yet his face was alight with joy as he looked round on the little group of disciples who sat at his feet, and as he laid his hand in loving welcome on the head of the tall, travel-stained newcomer.

"Draw near, and see for yourself, Luke. How often you have heard me speak of him. My brother in Christ, my beloved Epaphras from Asia."

The traveller turned to greet Luke, and as he did so, caught sight of the white-faced young man with the frightened haunted eyes in the doorway. They remained staring at each other in amazement for a few moments, and then Epaphras spoke.

"Can it be?" he said puzzled. "Were you not for many years in attendance on Philemon's crippled son? I heard you had perished in the Laodicean disaster. How comes it that I find you here?"

His voice was stern, and still Onesimus stood silent,

rooted to the spot. "Fool," cried his reason, "turn and run. There is yet time! Think of the penalties of the runaway slave. Think of those who, for the same crime, here in this city, have been branded, crucified, thrown to the beasts. What are you waiting for?"

"Those following Feet have all but caught up with you now," said his heart. "You are all but cornered and at bay. Now is your last chance to escape. But if you escape now, you escape for ever, and do you really want to escape?" So he stood his ground and answered humbly, "I am he. I escaped with my life and came to Rome. I have suffered many things and the burden of my guilt has become intolerable, so that I no longer desire life. I have been sick and would rest now; but later on in the evening, I pray that Master Paul will speak with me."

In truth, his head was swimming and the colour had drained from his face, leaving it ashen grey. He put out his hand to steady himself, and Luke was beside him in an instant. The doctor spread his own cloak on the floor and laid his patient down beside the Roman soldier. Onesimus closed his eyes and knew that this was the end. He was cornered and must turn and face up to the stern demands of love and bow to a new, Eternal Master. His brief, vain freedom was over.

But what these demands would be, he was too tired and weak to think out. He lay very still and at peace and listened to the conversation of the little group, the first news he had received of his home for two years.

They were speaking of the churches in Hierapolis, Laodicea and Colosse. All prospered, and Philemon and Apphia were well, strong in their love for Christ and for their brethren. Archippus had been sick and depressed, sometimes too tired to fulfil his ministry, yet battling on bravely; and now a joy had been given to him that he had never expected, for a tender attachment had grown up between him and a Christian maiden in Hierapolis. Yet the little Church was in danger, and Epaphras' voice was urgent and anxious as he spoke of the heresy that threatened it. There was that young Phrygian who was trying to combine the simplicity of the Gospel of Christ with their own pagan beliefs. Christian slaves had been partaking in strange rites, keeping feasts, fasting till they were pale and weak, and trying to rise by mortification of the flesh and a worship of angels to a gradual, painful knowledge of God.

"This heresy is not preached in Philemon's house," said Epaphras, "but it has subverted many and even drawn some away who used to gather there. It flatters their intellects and is not far removed from their own beliefs in spirit-worship and 'mysteries'."

"As though Christ were not all in all!" murmured the Apostle, visibly agitated. "I must write them a letter, begging them to beware, showing them again that in Christ dwells all the fulness of God. This is the only mystery they need ever explore."

The Roman guard was relieved by a great fierce brute of a man who sat with his back to the wall, scowling and picking his teeth. Paul greeted him courteously, and the talk flowed on, but Onesimus lost the thread. By the light of a smoky lamp he was watching the faces of the little company, urgent and troubled. There was a thin dedicated-looking young man called Timothy, whose eyes blazed with love as he watched the apostle, and another older man, called Epaphroditus, who seemed to be convalescing from a serious illness. A third, with Jewish features, sat humbly in the background and said very little - probably a servant, thought Onesimus sleepily and wondered how long they would all go on talking.

All night, he imagined, as another and another joined the group. A sharp-featured man called Demas came in and interrupted their discussions with news of what was happening in Rome. But no one else seemed very interested, and the talk veered back to heresy in the churches until a brother called Tychicus arrived. He had been preaching to a group of Christians in another district of Rome and seemed encouraged.

"We were a mixed company tonight," he said in a low voice, so as not to wake the soldier who was snoring loudly. "Slaves, Jews, a few of Caesar's household, two or three from the guard, high and low, Jew and Gentile, all one in Christ Jesus. But Aristobulus, who sees Nero almost daily, thinks that the storm will soon break in good earnest and that it is no longer safe to gather in private homes. He thinks we should find a more secret..."

Demas kicked him, and he broke off and looked round. He had not seen the stranger lying, apparently asleep, under the cloak in the shadows of the room. Onesimus, opening an eye, saw him stoop and trace that mysterious sign on the floor and saw the others shake their heads.

It was very late now. The company knelt round the dying lamp, and Paul prayed long and lovingly for the flock of God in Rome, in Greece, in Asia, for those threatened by ravening wolves in Colosse, for the burdened sinner sleeping on the floor. He blessed them as a father, and one by one they went off into the night, all except Timothy who stayed and brought the old man food and drink and would have settled him as comfortably as his chain would allow.

"Are you going to sleep, my father?"

"I think not, my son. I would speak with that boy who came tonight, if he is not asleep. Bring him to sup with us."

"I am not asleep," said Onesimus. He felt rested and ready to talk. He joined Paul and Timothy at their humble meal, and then, down on the dark floor, with his face hidden, he told the apostle all: his hatred of Archippus, his revenge at Ephesus, the years of theft, the culminating robbery and flight at Laodicea, the killing of his friend in the arena, and his final terror of death. Once he started, he felt he could never stop. All that had been locked in his angry, resentful, unhappy heart came flowing out that night like a black flood. Weary, Timothy lay down and slept, but Paul and Onesimus talked on.

Was there hope? Was there forgiveness? Would Christ yet have mercy in spite of the years of refusal and that determination to be free that had brought him so low? He asked these questions again and again, and Paul spoke to him long and earnestly about the Cross of Christ and all that it offered him.

"He can blot out that record of sin that is against you," said Paul. "He can take it out of the way, as though it were nailed to His Cross. Justified by faith, you can have peace with God. I know. I have trodden this path. I saw Stephen the martyr die, and I consented and guarded the clothes of those who stoned him. I knew that torment of conscience. But I will tell you, too, how I saw Christ."

It was almost morning when Paul finished that story.

Onesimus listened entranced. Truly how hard, how very hard, it had been to kick against the pricks. The guard stirred in his sleep. Onesimus lifted his eyes and saw the dawn stealing in through the bars of that prison room and felt as though he had been born again, a little child in a fair new world. The burden had been lifted for ever, and in the joy of sin forgiven he had barely, as yet, given a thought to the next step. Enough, for the moment, that he had come to Christ and Christ had received him.

Yet deep down in his broken, happy heart, lurked the question that Paul had asked on the Damascus road. Soon he must ask it, too, and find out the answer. "Lord, what wilt thou have me to do?"

22

HE FOUND A LODGING WITH THE JEW WHO had seemed like a servant, a man named John Mark, and he went daily to sit with the little company who surrounded Paul. He made himself useful, too, running errands, patching up the house, drawing water with his one arm; for John Mark was busy with some writing, and Timothy, who suffered from indigestion, was not used to hard, manual work. A timid, home-loving boy, Timothy's love for Paul had made him into a hero. He had followed him over land and sea, facing dangers and hardships; and now for two years he had shared the cheerless imprisonment. Onesimus grew to love Timothy, who never tired of telling him stories about the greatness and courage of his father in Christ.

Paul was very busy just then. Epaphroditus had travelled from Philippi some time previously to bring Paul a gift from the church, and he had lingered on, partly because he had become very ill, and partly because he could not bear to say goodbye. But summer was drawing to a close and if he wished to get home while the seas were still navigable he must leave very soon. Paul was busy composing and dictating a letter for him to take back to the Christians at Philippi.

It was costing him much thought and exercise of mind. The church at Philippi was very dear to him, and every memory of their faithfulness and love was precious. But they were not perfect. Lately, according to Epaphroditus, two or three of the women had been getting very quarrelsome, and Lydia, who had opened her wealthy home to the Christians, seemed unable to keep them in order. It was a difficult letter to write, and day after day he had dictated a little and prayed much, and Onesimus often sat listening, wondering at the loving exhortations and the gentle rebuke and at the amazing new trains of thought that the letter kept starting in his mind.

"I trust in the Lord Jesus to send Timothy unto you shortly."

Timothy, writing at Paul's dictation, looked up dismayed at the thought of going anywhere without his master; but Onesimus pricked up his ears. He loved Timothy, but Timothy acted as Paul's personal attendant. Epaphroditus would shortly be leaving for Philippi. Onesimus suddenly saw his own future stretching rosily before him. He would stay on in Timothy's place and look after Paul.

He smiled as he suddenly remembered the years he had spent loathing his slavery, yearning to be free of it. Now that he was free, he longed to be a bondslave to this decrepit, scarred old prisoner with the chain galling his wrist, and he suddenly realised what liberty really meant: freedom to bow to the dictates of love and to give yourself to its voluntary slavery. Apart from the discipline of love, freedom was a dreary wilderness without compass or direction, a desert full of mirages, promising everything but yielding nothing.

The more he thought about it, the better he liked the

idea. He had collected his money at the barracks, and though it was not as much as he had expected - the procurer had been in a towering passion at their feeble performance and obvious disinclination to kill each other - he had been able to pay his debts, secure his lodgings with John Mark, and he still had enough left to live on for some months. He had tried to buy some small luxuries for Paul, but the old man would not accept them. "Keep your money, my son," he had said gently. "Put it in safe deposit. I think, one day soon, you will need it."

What had he meant by that, wondered Onesimus; for he had a feeling that there was some hidden meaning in that apparently artless remark. But there was no opportunity to question Paul these days. There were always visitors waiting, and the old Apostle was absorbed in the departure of Epaphroditus and his letter to the Philippians. The seas were only considered perfectly safe till the middle of September; and Paul, well taught by his own experience of risking a journey too late in the year, was determined he should be gone by then. So he worked on, sometimes far into the night, his mind and heart more in Philippi than in Rome, till one day he reached the triumphant conclusion: "I have learned, in whatsoever state I am, therewith to be content. I know both how to be abased, and how to abound . . . to be full and to be hungry . . . I can do all things through Christ who strengtheneth me . . . I have all, and abound. But my God shall supply all your needs according to his riches in glory by Christ Jesus."

Even the guard, who knew a smattering of Greek, leaned forward and stared. Was this fellow a lunatic who had illusions? Sitting here, chained, huddled in an old patched cloak, with the threat of death hanging over his head, what on earth had he got to be content about? Onesimus, too, marvelled. Was it possible to accept any circumstances with joy if Christ were there? It seemed so. What a difference this would have made to his slavery, had he but known.

It was a sad day when Epaphroditus finally left. He did not know if he would ever see his dear, dear father in the faith again on earth; but to meet in the presence of Christ would be far better, and his eyes were bright with hope through his tears. Onesimus and the rest of the company went with him out along the Appian Way, for he was aiming for the port of Brundisium. They walked a long time in the bright September sunshine, with the vineyards a glory of gold on either side of them. At the top of a little hill, near the Jewish burial-ground, they finally committed Epaphroditus to God and said goodbye.

There was almost a feeling of relief as they met again by lamp-light that night. Soon the winter would come sweeping down from the Alps, and there could be no more serious partings until the spring. Paul looked tenderly round on the little group.

"I must write letters to the believers in the Lycus valley this winter," he said. "God will give me the words I need. Tychicus, when the winter is over, you shall set out to visit the churches in Asia. It may even be that I shall accompany you. Surely my trial cannot be delayed much longer now."

The days sped by in work and learning, but there was unrest in the air. The wickedness of the Emperor's new favourite, Tigellinus, and Nero's terror of any rival loyalty to himself were making the position of the Christians in the royal household almost impossible. Virtue itself was suspect, and to worship Christ was considered treachery.

A meeting was held one night, and elders of different groups in Rome crowded into Paul's room with tense anxious faces.

"The houses are watched and we no longer dare sing our hymns," they insisted. "Arrests may be made any day, and there will be neither mercy nor justice at the trial of a Christian. We must find some secret place of meeting outside the city. Some have suggested those old subterranean Jewish burial places out on the Appian Way. If some of us could go by night and continue these excavations, then in any time of danger we could gather there in safety. None would hear us down there in the dungeons of the earth."

The company nodded. It seemed a wise plan, and Onesimus rejoiced. He was longing to use his muscles, and here was a chance to put his tremendous strength at the service of the Church as soon as his arm was healed. He was eager to start, and he talked to John Mark about it when they reached their lodging late that night. John Mark smiled. "It would be an excellent thing for you, Onesimus," he said, "and would work off some of your spare energy. But I shall not join you. I have to finish my task."

"What is your task, John Mark?" asked Onesimus timidly.

John Mark was a shy, humble man who talked little about his own affairs; he was usually hidden away in a corner, writing. But when he wrote his dark eyes glowed, and he seemed to be transformed into a different being. Now, he hesitated. "Have you ever wondered how I, a Jew from Jerusalem, came to be here with Paul in Rome?" he asked abruptly.

"I supposed," replied Onesimus, "that you came with him on his travels. Has he not been in Jerusalem many times?"

John Mark shook his head. "I will tell you my story," he said, bringing the words out with difficulty, "because in some ways it started like yours. It started more than thirty years ago, when I was just a boy. My mother had a big, spacious house in Jerusalem, near the palace of the High Priest, and she often ministered to Jesus Christ. I loved Him too, but I was very young. It was the Passover night, and we all knew something terrible was going to happen. We had been keeping the feast, and it was late before we went to bed. Then we heard a great noise in the night, an armed rabble passing under the window, and I looked out and saw Him - pushed along captive in the midst, and His disciples following some way behind. I thought this was the chance of my life to stand with them, or rather with Him. I had always longed to be one of His disciples. I wrapped a cloth round me and rushed out into the night to catch them up. But just before I arrived, He had said something that had angered everybody. I think He asked them, quite calmly, why they had never arrested Him before. The disciples, seeing the mob getting threatening, all turned and ran."

There was a long silence. Onesimus reclined on his couch; Mark sat with his head in his hands, struggling to go on.

"I ran too. I was suddenly terrified. They seized hold

of the cloth I had wrapped round me, but I shook free and left it in their hands. Later I tried to peep into the courtyard of the Palace, and to my relief I saw Peter in there. It was nearly morning then, and I remember hearing a cock crow. But as he approached, Peter suddenly threw back his head and cursed and swore and said he had never known Jesus before, and that broke whatever I had left. I went home and did not dare leave the house for three days. John was the only disciple who was with Him when He died. I felt life was over for me. I lived on in Jerusalem and worked as a scribe and saw a lot of the apostles, especially Peter. He told me a great deal about the years he had spent with the Master, and I felt sadder than ever that I had missed my chance. I became very friendly with my cousin, Barnabas. Thirteen years after that night, he took me up to Antioch with him, and there I had my second chance."

Onesimus looked up eagerly.

"No, it is nothing to be glad about. I failed again. I had not got it in me to succeed. Barnabas and Paul were sent out by the Church to preach the Gospel to the Gentiles. I went with them, pleased and proud to have the chance to serve Christ once more and to make good. But I was frightened of those Jews and of that awful sorcerer in Cyprus, and when we crossed to Perga I was seasick all the way. I was a town boy and those wild snow-tipped heights that rise from the coasts terrified me. Paul was going to plunge straight into their fastnesses, north to Lystra. I felt sure we should be attacked by brigands or eaten by wolves. My nerves gave way completely and I turned and went home."

There was another long silence. The moonlight

suddenly flooded the little room and rested on Mark's head like a benediction.

"By the time I reached Jerusalem, I regretted it bitterly. I thought my heart would break. When they returned two years later, wounded and scarred with stoning, I dared to ask for another chance, but Paul would not hear of it. I was a deserter, a failure, and there was no room for such in Christ's army. Barnabas thought he was hard and unjust, and he took me back to Cyprus and was very good to me; but I think Paul was right. Christ Himself said that those who put their hand to the plough and then look back are not fit for the kingdom of God."

"And then?" queried Onesimus.

"It was something that Peter told me that gave me hope. I had always wondered how he could preach after he had denied Jesus like that; and when I was feeling particularly hopeless one night, I asked him about it. He told me that after he had denied Jesus, he turned and saw his Master gazing at him, and that broke his heart. He gave up everything and went back to his fishing, feeling that life with Christ was finished. But one morning his risen Master came down to the beach very early and lit a fire just as they were coming in with their nets. And just as Peter had denied Him three times by that fire in the dark, so the Lord sat by that other fire at dawn and gave him the chance to take back all he had said. Three times He made Peter say that he loved Him, as though his love could wipe out his lies. But he had to go back to the point where he had failed, and unsay it.

"There is not much more," said Mark, "But I thought perhaps I could do the same. I had left Paul when he was in danger and needed me, and when I heard he was in prison, awaiting trial and possibly death, I decided to come to Him and to stand by Him to the end, if need be. He was very kind and received me and forgave the past. There is not much to do here, except to wait, so I am trying to write down all that Peter told me about those three years. It seems right to me that I, the servant who failed and turned back, should tell the story of God's Servant who never turned back. Sometimes when I write about Him, I feel that I am one with Him, carried forward to my goal. I feel that He will somehow finish all that I have failed in, and that in Him I may yet accomplish some good thing."

Onesimus had risen from his elbow. "John Mark," he asked hoarsely, "why do you tell me all this?"

"Because," said John Mark steadily, "I do not think there is any progress until we go back to the place where we failed and seek to put it right."

He lay down to sleep, but Onesimus tossed and turned on his bed. To go back to where he had failed and put it right! Back to slavery, back to disgrace and punishment! Was it all to end in this?

And not only slavery. One night, sitting in the dark so that no one should see his flaming cheeks, he had dared to asked Master Epaphras whether he had heard any news of the little orphaned Mistress Eirene, and Epaphras had answered with tender amusement. She had refused all proposals of marriage from rich suitors and was still single and free. Despite her gentle birth and high position, she had insisted on staying on with her father's shepherd and his wife who taught her of Christ and brought her into the Church at Laodicea. She lived as a shepherdess and had spent much of her inheritance on children who, like herself, were left homeless and orphaned in the earthquake.

As a Christian and a free man, Onesimus might go back and claim her; as a slave, never. Christ was a hard Master, and yet Paul and Mark and Timothy had never sought to be free of His service. To go forward was anguish. To turn back was unthinkable.

He buried his face in the pillow, and Paul's question was wrung from his aching heart, "Lord, what wilt thou have me to do?"

23

IT WAS A BRIGHT MAY MORNING, SOME months later, when two travellers passed beneath the walls of Laodicea and left the town behind them. They walked slowly, Tychicus because he was getting on in years and was coming to the end of a long journey, and Onesimus because his heart was heavy as lead.

It seemed years since that morning when they had said goodbye to Paul, still in chains, his trial apparently forgotten by the irresponsible knave who called himself Emperor. Paul was hopeful, sure that he would soon be set at liberty and come to them. But Onesimus could feel no such hope, and when the day of parting came he felt his heart would break.

All the beauty of the Italian spring, with its foaming fruit blossom and fields of asphodel and narcissi and iris, had failed to cheer him, and the long sea journey with its idle hours had been torture to him. They had stayed for a week or so in Ephesus, and the Christians, pressing on in spite of the riots and persecutions, had greeted them joyfully and had gathered night after night to hear and discuss the letter Paul had written to them. It was a long circular letter which was to be read again in Hierapolis, Laodicea and Colosse; and the words of that letter had steadied Onesimus and brought some measure of light and comfort. Now that he had irrevocably renounced his earthly love, it was good to be reminded of the love of

Christ that passeth knowledge; and in battling against his fear and rebellion, it was comforting to hear of the helmet of salvation, the shield of faith and the sword of the Spirit. And now, although his heart ached and his lips felt dry with fear, he was conscious of a strange peace. He had obeyed, and the results of his obedience he could leave with his Master.

"I think we shall be there soon after noon," said Tychicus, glancing at the steep little road that led up into the hills from the right of the highway. "I shall be glad to rest for a while in Colosse. It has been a long journey."

"You will read them the letters tonight, Master Tychicus?" said Onesimus, slowing his pace, for the older man seemed weary.

"I think the Christians will gather tonight to read Paul's letter to the church at Colosse. I pray that they may take it to heart. The Ephesian letter can wait, for it is more general in character and addressed to all. The third one is merely personal, and deals with a private matter."

"The third one?" queried Onesimus, surprised. "I did not know you carried three letters."

"Yes, a personal one from Paul to Philemon. It is not to be read in the church. It deals with some matter that concerns him alone."

They climbed on in silence for a time. Soon they would reach the lower plain and then Onesimus would look up and see the outskirts of Colosse and the canyons and the meadows, bright with marigolds and daisies, where Philemon's sheep grazed. Already he could hear the crying of the half-grown lambs, the bleating of the dams and the rushing of the stream where he had loved to play as a little boy. How he had sometimes longed for these sights and sounds in Rome! Now, they only filled him with dread and foreboding.

"Christ," he whispered, "give me courage and let not my punishment be more than I can bear." And once again some words from the Ephesian letter came back to him and sang themselves to the steady rhythm of their footsteps all the way up the hill: 'Able to do... able to do... abundantly, above all that we ask or think.'

They were climbing the second hill, taking the path that by-passed the town and led up to the farm at the foot of the canyons. In the shade of a tall poplar tree Onesimus stopped.

"Master Tychicus," he said, "you go on alone. I will wait here under the tree. Tell Master Philemon that I have come, repentant, forgiven by Christ, to return to my slavery and to hear what punishment he thinks meet to inflict. If he will receive me, beg him of his mercy to speak to me here alone."

Tychicus hesitated, and Onesimus read his thoughts.

"I will not run away, Master Tychicus," he said. "Have I followed Christ thus far, to turn back now? My Master will certainly find me waiting here."

"Very well, my son," replied Tychicus, and he went on alone. Onesimus watched him disappear into the homestead and then, burying his head in his hands, he sat and waited. He wondered whether Philemon would deign to come himself. It was unlikely. He would probably send a couple of slaves to chain and lead him in as befitted a runaway thief. Well, whatever was coming, he was ready for it, because Christ would stand beside him. Once again he was conscious of that unreasonable sense of peace.

Footsteps were approaching. Not the hurried footsteps of slaves, but the slow, halting footsteps he knew so well. He could not look up; for this was going to be the worst ordeal of all.

"Onesimus!" Archippus' hand was on his shoulder. "You've come back? Glaucus told us you were dead, and how I have mourned for you. I heard Tychicus telling my father. I think he will come soon, but I could not wait. I slipped out while they were talking. Oh, Onesimus, how glad I am to see you!"

"You won't be when you know the truth," blurted out Onesimus, "and I might as well tell you right away. Archippus, it was all because of me you became a cripple. I hated you and I whispered to the crowd that your father had burnt the books. I did not mean you to be really hurt - just a black eye - but I started it. You would be walking straight and strong today, if it had not been for me."

There was a stunned silence. It took Archippus some moments to digest this news. Then he gave a shaky little laugh.

"You had reason to hate me, Onesimus. I wronged you and humiliated you not just that once, but every day. If I had not become a cripple, I should still be walking in arrogance and sin. I sometimes think I am like Jacob at the ford of Jabbok. I had to halt upon my thigh before I could know His Name. I'm still glad you have come home."

They were silent again, Archippus because he had no more to say, and Onesimus because he was overwhelmed with love and gratitude and relief. Then Archippus suddenly whispered, "My father!"

He was coming down the hill slowly, tall and dignified as ever, with a parchment in his hand. Onesimus rose to meet him and then bowed himself to the ground.

"Rise," said Philemon. "We counted you as dead and mourned for you. I presume you took the money and fled to Rome. Tell me, why have you returned?"

"To confess and atone for my sin, which is greater than you know; to restore what I can of your gold, and to put myself once again into your hands, as your slave and your property, to do what you will with me."

"That is good," said Philemon, "but you have not really answered my question. *Why* did you come back?"

"Because Christ bade me come. At first I resisted His voice, but I found no rest; so I came."

"You did well. Be seated, and you too, my son, Archippus. I have a letter from our dear father in Christ, Paul. Let us read it together."

It was very quiet on the hillside. Even the lambs seemed to have stopped their bleating as the gracious words that have survived the centuries fell for the first time on the amazed ears of the guilty slave.

"Paul, a prisoner of our Lord Jesus Christ ... unto Philemon our dearly-beloved ... I beseech thee for my son Onesimus whom I have begotten in my bonds, who in time past was to thee unprofitable, but now profitable to thee and to me ... Receive him not now as a servant, but above a servant, a brother beloved ... Receive him as myself. If he hath wronged thee, or oweth thee ought, put that on mine account; I Paul have written it with mine own hand, I will repay it."

The letter drew to a close.

"So this is your writing of emancipation," said

Philemon with a smile. "I could not refuse him anything. Onesimus, I grant you your pardon and freedom for Paul's sake. You shall enter my house, not as a slave, but as a brother in Christ, truly now twice freed."

• • • •

'Above all that you ask or think' - those were the words that sang in his ears as he bounded down the hill three days later, long before sunrise. The first birds seemed to be shouting hallelujah, and the stream to be bubbling its praise for its creator. 'Ye shall go out with joy and be led forth with peace. The mountains and the hills shall break forth before you into singing and all the trees of the field shall clap their hands.' The words had been written centuries before; but had anyone ever gone forth on a yet dark summer morning with such joy as his?

The miles swept past. He was walking in at the gates of Laodicea, marvelling at the work they had accomplished in the past three years. Fair buildings were beginning to rise from orderly streets where ruins and heaps of rubble had lain. It was said that Rome had sent an offer of help to the afflicted town; but the citizens of Laodicea were entirely self-sufficient. "We are rich and increased in goods, and have need of nothing," they had replied proudly.

He had reached the Hierapolis gate, now restored, and there he stopped, suddenly transfixed. She was coming up the slope towards the city, walking slowly because three or four little children were clinging to her hands and her skirts. The sun had swung clear of the eastern heights, and its first light fell on her bent head, and the flowers were opening their faces as though to look up at her. The silver dew still lay thick on the grass. It might have been the first morning in Eden, thought the boy in the gateway.

"There is a man waiting for you!" said one of the children. She looked up quickly. Apart from the flush of her cheeks and the brightening of her eyes, she showed no surprise. After all, in a sense, he had been there all the time. She quickened her pace and came straight to him, and the little children ran to keep up with her, leaving tiny footprints in the dew.

"Grace and peace be with you, Mistress Eirene," he said gently. "I have kept my word and come back to you, a free man and a follower of Christ."

She looked up at him, and her face was radiant as the morning. "I knew you would come," she said. And, gathering the children about them, they turned their backs on the town and set out hand in hand towards the sunrising and the hills of Hierapolis.

Look out for other titles by
Patricia St. John:

A Home for Virginia
ISBN 1-85792-961-6
978-1-85792-961-4

A Young Person's Guide
to Knowing God

Hardback: ISBN 1-85792-600-5
978-1-85792-600-2
Paperback: ISBN 1-85792-558-0
978-1-85792-558-6

Talking & Listening to God
ISBN 1-85792-840-7
978-1-85792-840-2

The Safe Place
ISBN 1-85792-779-6
978-1-85792-779-5

LIGHT KEEPERS

Look out for our series
written by Irene Howat:

Ten Boys who Made History:
ISBN 1-85792-836-9 * 978-1-85792-836-5
Ten Girls who Made History:
ISBN 1-85792-837-7 * 978-1-85792-837-2
Ten Girls who Didn't Give In:
ISBN 1-84550-036-9 * 978-1-84550-036-8
Ten Boys who Didn't Give In:
ISBN 1-84550-035-0 * 978-1-84550-035-1
Ten Boys who Changed the World:
ISBN 1-85792-579-3 * 978-1-85792-579-1
Ten Girls who Changed the World:
ISBN 1-85792-649-8 * 978-1-85792-649-1
Ten Boys who Made a Difference:
ISBN 1-85792-775-3 * 978-1-85792-775-7
Ten Girls who Made a Difference:
ISBN 1-85792-776-1 * 978-1-85792-776-4